TABLE OF CONTENTS

VOLUME THREE
FLORIDA WRITERS ASSOCIATION

the Peppertree Press
Sarasota, Florida

For information regarding permission,
call 941-922-2662 or contact us at our website:
www.peppertreepublishing.com or write to:
the Peppertree Press, LLC.
Attention: Publisher
1269 First Street, Suite 7
Sarasota, Florida 34236

ISBN: 978-1-61493-062-4
Library of Congress Number: 2011939051
Printed in the U.S.A.
Printed October 2011

ACKNOWLEDGEMENTS

FWA's Collection #3 – Let's Talk is the third book in a series of short stories written by Florida Writers Association members. Even though we call them short stories, not all are actually fiction. Among the winners are some nonfiction and some snippets of memoir.

Writing is a sharing experience, but it can also be a learning experience. When you write to a theme, it stretches you as a writer. That was the purpose of this year's contest. To stretch our writing skills by using a format not familiar to everyone. All of our entrants succeeded admirably! The entries were funny, cute, sad, and some made me cry, but all were worthy. Thank you!

Well over two hundred entries poured in from FWA members everywhere. They were posted without author name to a specially designed website accessible only by our judges. Huge thanks to Shara Smock, FWA's Regional Director for Brevard County, for taking on the additional volunteer responsibility of receiving and posting these entries. Shara Smock also collected our finalists' photos and bios.

The websites produced for viewing the stories and entering judges' votes were created and maintained by Karen Lieb, President of Florida Writers Foundation. Karen's also FWA's official photographer, and further helped by formatting the pictures for publication. Thank you, Butterfly.

Our anonymous judges read and scored the entries. FWA is deeply indebted to them, and thanks each for their time, dedication, and willingness to volunteer for this worthwhile project.

Each finalist's entry is presented as entered, with no editing. Many of the entrants took advantage of either attending one of FWA's many Critique Groups across the state, or using FWA's Editing Service, which offered special pricing. The quality of entries reflects the professionalism of our members.

It is with heartfelt gratitude that FWA acknowledges W. Bruce Cameron's contribution to this publication. He had perhaps the hardest job of all . . . picking only ten to be his favorites out of the truly wonderful winning stories.

Finally, our sincere thanks to Julie Ann Howell and Teri Franco of Peppertree Press from FWA's Board of Directors for graciously donating all publishing costs for this project. Their patience and expertise throughout the formatting of the manuscript was invaluable.

Chrissy Jackson,
President, FWA

Vicki Morgan and Racquel Henry,
FWA Collections Coordinators

New York Times Bestselling Author

W. Bruce Cameron

A
DOG'S
PurPose

A Novel for Humans

"Anyone who has ever loved a dog needs
to read this wise, touching, often hilarious novel."

**Dr. Marty Becker, resident veterinarian
on *Good Morning America***

INTRODUCTION

I have been a writer nearly my whole life, but none of it would have happened if it hadn't been for what are rather awkwardly called, "dialogue tags." Literally, dialogue tags are the "he said, she said" of storytelling, the part no one ever says in a movie, or in real life, for that matter. But they can be magic.

I was in fourth grade when a simple assignment changed me forever. All we had to do was come up with ten different words to fill in the blank in the following sentence:

"Get out," he _____."

Just in case we were too dense to understand what we were being asked to do, the teacher provided us with an example.

"Get out," he *said*.

Hmmm… that's the one I was planning to use. Okay, how about shouted?

"Get out," he shouted.

Nine more to go. Oh, how about,

"Get out," he sobbed.

And then I stopped, stunned by what had just happened. I hadn't just changed the word, I had changed the *story*. When he shouted he was angry, but now he was sobbing—something tragic had just occurred!

"Get out," he laughed.

Is he laughing because it's funny? Or is it a mocking laugh, an "I-run-this-place-now-so-get-out" laugh. I wanted to know more. What was going on? Who were these people? Get out of *what*?

There was only one way get the answers to any of these questions: I had to write them.

And that's what I've been doing ever since.

So how did I feel about a compilation of stories that were, by design, to have no dialogue tags at all? Where the characters would be inferred by their words, where inflection would have to lie within the cadence of the sentence and not be propped up with laughter, sobbing, or shouting?

I thought it would be fun to try, and to see what other people came up with along the way. It's called writing, and it's what I've been compelled to do since fourth grade. Practicing the craft. Flexing the storytelling muscles.

So read on. Enjoy. Don't worry, we're not doing away with dialogue tags entirely, or forever.

Remember, they're *magic*.

W. Bruce Cameron
2011

Tech Support for Mom

"Hi Bruce, your dad and I want to watch a DVD. We finally agreed on one. Wait, hang on. *What? You said you wanted to watch it! Well I don't know what it's about, I haven't seen it! For heaven's sake.* Now he says he doesn't want to watch it."

"Well Mom, thanks for the update."

"Whether he watches it or not, I'm going to watch it and I can't remember how to make the DVD player work."

"Oh, okay. Is the DVD player on?"

"Should I turn it on?"

"Yes, that would probably help."

"Okay. Do I use the DVD remote or the TV remote?"

"The DVD remote."

"Or, what's this? This is the cable remote."

"The DVD remote."

"Is this… there's another one here, what's this one?"

"Use the DVD remote."

"Why do we have so many remotes?"

"Use the DVD remote."

"Okay. The DVD remote. What button do I push?"

"The one that says power."

"Okay, I pushed it."

"What happened?"

"The lights went out on the DVD player."

"Oh, okay, that means it was already on. Push the button again."

"I don't remember turning it on."

"Push the button again."

"Would I have had to turn it on to put in the DVD?"

"Yes. Push the button again."

"Okay, I did. The lights came on and then went off."

"Did you push the button twice?"

"I did what you told me."

"Okay, push the button again."

"*Again?*"

"Push the button again."

"Okay."

"Do you see lights on the DVD player?"

"Yes."

"And what do you see on the TV?"

"A duck."

"A duck?"

"Or maybe a goose. Some sort of animated thing. Duck, goose, it's animated."

"Is it the movie you wanted to watch?"

"No! You mean the duck? That's really funny. No, the movie has Al Pacino. Is that his name?"

"Okay. Get the TV remote."

"Do you ever watch this? You like animation."

"Mom. How can I know what show you're watching? I can't see what's on your TV."

"Well I can't either."

"You can't see it?"

"I mean I don't know what show it is."

"Point the TV remote at the TV and push the button that says Menu."

"Okay. Whoa! Now there's text all over the screen!"

"Those are menu selections. What do they say?"

"Well I don't know."

"What do you mean?"

"When I saw the words I pushed the menu button again and they went away."

"Why did you push the menu button twice?"

"You had me push the DVD button twice."

"You're right. Okay. Push the menu button once, then read me the words you see."

"It says, Signal, External Input...."

"External Input. Highlight External Input and push Select."

"Okay. Whoa!"

"What happened?"

"The dog just about knocked me over."

"Are you okay?"

"Of course."

"Did you push select?"

"I can't remember."

"What does it say on the screen?"

"Nothing."

"Nothing? Did you push menu again?"

"No. Let me ask your father."

"Wait, why?"

"He took the remote. He said he was getting impatient. *Bill! Do you want to watch the movie or not?*"

"Was he able to get the DVD working, then?"

"He says he doesn't care if we watch the movie. But I do. It's got that actor in it, Mel Gibson. Do you like him? He was so good in *Da Vinci Code*."

"He... you mean Tom Hanks?"

"Who? Was he in the Godfather movies?"

"No, that was Al Pacino."

"What did I say?"

"You said Mel Gibson."

"Well that's not what I meant. Who played Indiana Jones?"

"That was Harrison Ford."

"Okay, not him."

"Mom, why don't you either hand the phone to Dad or have him give you the remote back."

"*Bill, if you want to watch the movie you have to give me the remote.*"

"Okay, Mom? Do you have the remote?"

"Denzel. That's who."

"Denzel Washington?"

"Who?"

"What?"

"You just said it was Denzel and I asked if you meant Denzel Washington."

"For what?"

"Mom. You… Okay, do you have the remote?"

"Yes!"

"Hi Mom, so what's on the screen now?"

"The movie!"

"What? You got the DVD player working? How?"

"I don't know, I was just pushing buttons."

"Well if you don't know how you did it, how will you watch DVDs in the future?"

"Oh, that's simple, I'll just call you!"

W. Bruce Cameron

W. Bruce Cameron is the NY Times bestselling author several novels, including *A Dog's Purpose* and *Emory's Gift*. His book *8 Simple Rules for Dating my Teenage Daughter* was made into the ABC TV series of the same name, starring the late John Ritter. *A Dog's Purpose* will be released as a live action film from DreamWorks in 2012. In June 2011, Cameron was voted Newspaper Columnist of the Year by the National Society of Newspaper Columnists. Cameron is currently at work on his next novel; his dog is currently at work digging a hole in the living room carpet.

Greave Contact

"Nurse Mitchell! Bring the patient into emergency bay one, stat!"

"Doctor Yorick, I found contact information in the patient's purse; I'll call now."

"Great, we need it quickly. Techs—get me a chest x-ray, full blood panel, and a CT of the head. Get that blood now people, clock's ticking!"

◆

"Hello, this is Nurse Mitchell from Stone View Memorial Hospital in Nashua. May I please speak with Jack Greave?"

"He's not here at the moment, maybe I can help you. I'm his wife Joy."

"Do you expect him anytime soon, Mrs. Greave?"

"No, well, I have no idea really, why? What is this about?"

"I'm sorry to tell you, his mother was brought into the emergency room twenty minutes ago, she's been in a very serious accident and we need his authorization for possible surgery."

"What type of surgery?"

"We don't know at this point, she is still being evaluated, but we need to proceed quickly if necessary. Can you contact him for us?"

"How *did* you get our phone number?"

"Excuse me?"

"Our number, did *she* tell you to call?"

"No, Mrs. Greave, she is presently unresponsive, she had the emergency contact information in her wallet, and she noted *only* your husband was to be called."

"I see."

"Mrs. Greave, I must insist you contact him if possible, the sooner the better."

"So is it that serious? Is she going to die?"

"I'm sorry we don't know her complete condition just yet, but we're doing our best to help her."

"Well thank you for the call Nurse--?"

"Mitchell."

"Yes, Nurse Mitchell. I'll try to get in touch with my husband now, and then I'll head over to the hospital to do what I can."

"Thank you Mrs. Greave, goodbye."

◆

"Doctor Yorick, I spoke with Jack Greave's wife, Joy. She will try to reach her husband. How is Mrs. Greave?"

"*You called Joy? That is the bitch who hit me! Ran me down like a dog in my own driveway, she left me there to die! I was on my way to tell Jack and she tried to kill me. Oh please, get my son now! I have to tell him.*"

"Her CT scan shows an acute subdural hematoma. She's stable for now, but we may need to drill the skull to relieve the pressure on her brain, we need the consent form signed before we can proceed."

"Mrs. Greave? Can you hear me? This is Nurse Mitchell, if you can hear me squeeze my hand."

"*Yes, yes, I hear you. Help me. My head hurts. Oh please, do something. This thing in my throat burns, is that why you can't hear me?*"

"Nothing Doctor, she isn't responding."

"*I'm here! Help me! Call the police!*"

"I doubt her condition is going to change anytime soon. They need you in back in the emergency room; she'll be monitored from the desk. Please go. Dr. Black will take over for me, I'm going home."

"Home, you're going home? What about me? Oh God, please get Jack."

"Nurse, please, emergency room."

"Yes, Doctor. Have a nice evening."

✦

"Hi Jack."

"Joy— is anything wrong? You know I'm in meetings all afternoon, and then I'm catching the six o'clock flight out to L.A."

"No, nothing's wrong, in fact everything is great here. I ran into someone while I was on an errand and I thought about you. I wanted to say how much I'm going to miss you. Two weeks is a long time."

"Ah, Joy, you'll be fine. I've been away lots of times and you seem to keep yourself occupied. Just do me a favor and check on Mother sometime this week will you? She acted a little strange the other night when she was over for dinner. Did you say anything to upset her?"

"No, I don't think so. She's a little paranoid you know, getting crazy thoughts in her head. I don't think she trusts me with her checking account. I'm only trying to help her with her finances, remember how late she was on her payments a few months ago? I think her mind is going, plus she keeps losing things."

"Yes, I remember. I appreciate your caring. Try not to get angry about her lack of gratitude, since dad died she's been a little depressed. You're the best daughter-in-law anyone could ask for."

"Let's not forget about best lover, too."

"Right—I'll call you tomorrow, love you."

"Love you too, bye."

✦

"Pierce, this is Joy, I'll have your money tomorrow. Meet me at nine in the hotel parking lot."

"Yeah, better be sure you do sweetie pie, it would be a shame to ruin your *perfect* marriage."

"Twenty thousand and you keep your mouth shut forever. Nine a.m."

✦

"Good evening Nurse, is the intensive care unit on this floor? I'm looking for my mother-in-law, Mrs. Eleanor Greave."

"Yes ma'am. She's in room number three- thirteen down the hall on the left. She is still unconscious and likely won't hear you, although holding her hand can't hurt. I'm afraid you can only stay ten minutes."

"Thank you Nurse. Ten minutes is plenty of time for what I have to say."

◆

"Hello, Mother dear. You don't look very well."

"Joy? Oh no, get out! Nurse! Help me! Help me!

"I see you're still hanging on, you tough old bird. It probably won't be long now though. I came by to tell you thanks."

"Thanks for what, not leaving a dent on your hood?"

"It *seems* you took the better part of your savings out of the bank just yesterday. Do you have a young lover who is blackmailing *you*, too? That's very naughty Eleanor—a woman your age. What would Jack say?"

"You stole my money?! Now you're a thief and a slut! Where's Jack? I knew you were screwing around... Wait until he finds out who you are... What you are... He'll leave you... faster... than you drive that... Porsche you..."

"I'll tell you what he'll say Eleanor—nothing. He'll never find out what I've done and he'll be speechless by your careless money handling, losing thousands of dollars in such a short time. Jack is flying to Los Angeles, right now in fact. He has no idea you're in the hospital and by the time he finds out, you'll be dead I'm afraid, so sad."

"Chest...hurts..."

"Doctor Black to room three-thirteen—code blue."

"Please step outside Mrs. Greave. You're mother-in-law is in cardiac arrest."

"Of course doctor, please do what you can to save her."

◆

"Jack darling, I'm so sorry to leave a message like this. There's been a terrible accident, it's your Mother. I'm at the hospital, I'm afraid we've lost her honey, I'm sorry, she's gone—"

"Paddles— stand back, and... clear!—"
"We have rhythm doctor— she's back!"

DOREEN L. MYERS

Doreen L. Myers recently rediscovered her love of writing, after attending a life story writing workshop in 2006. Since then, she has become an active participant in several writing groups and is currently writing her first novel. Relocating from Pennsylvania in 1993, she and her husband David live in Valrico.

Traffic Stop

"Evening, Officer. Why'd you stop my wife? Was she speeding?"

"Step away, Sir."

"Officer, that's my wife in that car. I've been following her home and I'm concerned."

"Nothing for you to be concerned about. Step away."

"I was right behind her. I know she wasn't speeding."

"Sir. You are interfering with official police business. Get back in your car and get out of here!"

"Officer, I have a right to know why you stopped my wife!"

"You been drinking tonight?"

"I don't drink alcohol."

"All drunks say that. You are under arrest. Put your hands on the hood of her car and spread your legs."

"That hurt!"

"Tell the desk sergeant Officer Cooper kicked you in the ankles. Now give me your right arm . . . your left."

"Oww!"

"Got anything in your pockets I should be concerned about? Weapons? Drugs?"

"Of course not!"

"What've we got here? Handkerchief . . . keys . . . change . . . wallet. Twenty four dollars in bills. I'm gonna check your driver's license."

"Go ahead."

"Roger Mayhew? My, my. You really are her husband. What a surprise. Where's your car?"

"Right there."

"If I search it what will I find?"

"A spare tire?"

"Wise guy, huh? . . . Have a seat on the curb."

" . . . Roger. Honey. Sweetie . . . Look up here . . . Look at me . . . Be nice to Officer Cooper. You are scaring me with your behavior."

"I just wanted to make sure you're safe."

"Shut up. I can't hear myself talking on the radio . . . Dispatch? . . . Officer Cooper. My 10-20 is the top of Millers Hill. Southbound . . . a 10-60 . . . That's right, traffic stop, but I got a situation. I need a 10-16 . . . What do you mean you don't know what's a 10-16. Didn't they teach you at the academy? . . . It's prisoner transport, for the love of . . . And send a tow truck. Cooper out . . ."

"All right, mister, sit tight. And while we wait for your ride, I'll go back and talk to the young lady—if that's okay by you . . ."

◆

"Hey, that was quick."

"What you got Coop?"

"Well if it ain't Frick and Frack."

"Cut the crap Cooper. What's going on?"

"Drunk claims he's the lady's husband."

"He isn't?"

"His driver's license is probably fake and he's interfering with my investigation. Take him to the station and run the breathalyzer on him."

"Sure Coop. Sammy and I will take good care of him."

"Yeah—yeah. You two should get married. You'd make a nice couple."

"Up yours Cooper . . . All right Sir, on your feet, and watch your head getting in the car . . . Easy does it. . . Now sit back and relax. . .

Okay, Sammy, let's go."

"Officers. I've never been arrested and I'm concerned. That cop stopped my wife without a good reason and I'm supposed to relax? I'm not a criminal and I can't sit back with my hands cuffed in back."

"It's only a short ride to the station. Officer Cooper stopped you because you've been drinking."

"I haven't had a drop in ages. I stopped because Officer Cooper stopped my wife."

"That was your wife? Looks like Cooper's up to his old tricks. Sammy, should we let Mister Mayhew in on the secret? . . . You think yes? . . . O.K. Here we go . . . Cooper thinks he's God's gift to women. He stops only the pretty ones, telling them he'll tear up their ticket if they'll go on a date with him. Now he's ticked at you for messing up his plan."

"That's extortion."

"That it is. I wouldn't do anything like that, and neither would Sammy here. But then Sammy never stood a chance with the ladies either . . . He got hit with the ugly stick when he was a baby. Girls, girls, as far as the eye can see, but does Sammy score? Hell no."

"Your mother wears combat boots."

"Aww . . . You hurt me right here, Sammy. Right here in the heart. Oh, never mind. Here we are . . . I'll take Mister Mayhew into the station ."

◆

"Hallo Sergeant. I brought you somebody so you won't feel so useless and lonesome on the midnight shift. This here's Mister Roger Mayhew. Take care of him."

"Sure thing Jack . . . Will do."

"Good night Sergeant and goodbye Mister Mayhew."

"All right, Sir. Turn around so I can take your cuffs off, fingerprint you and take your picture."

"Fingerprints? Pictures? Don't you have to give me my Miranda Warning?"

"You've been watching too much television . . . Where's the arrest report? . . . Ah, Officer Cooper's work . . . DUI arrest. Have we been imbibing too many adult beverages, Mister Mayhew?"

"I don't know about you, but I don't drink and I am going to file charges against Officer Cooper."

"Yeah, yeah. Good luck with that. Empty your pockets and hand me your watch. I'll put you in a holding cell. Somebody will get you for the breathalyzer test."

" . . . Mister Mayhew? . . . I see Officer Cooper got you on a DUI. First, we'll do an inebriation test and then the breathalyzer."

"I don't drink."

"Sure thing, Sir. Tell me, what time is it?"

"What time? How should I know? You guys took my watch."

"I wouldn't get smart with me if I were you. Now stand up and without moving your head follow the tip of my pen with your eyes . . . Hmm . . . Once more. O.K. . . . Let's do the dum-dum test."

"The dum-dum test?"

"Breathalyzer. Dumb drunks think they can fool it; never can. Follow me . . . Careful, Sir. Here we are. Sit down. Officer Geller will be with you in a minute. He's a licensed and certified breathalyzer operator."

"Good. Let's get this over with."

"All done, Mister Mayhew, but I want to show the results to my shift supervisor . . . Sergeant?"

"Yes Geller?"

"Mister Mayhew here blew zero alcohol, but he's Cooper's collar and he's complaining."

"Cooper's collar? Zero alcohol? . . . Mister Mayhew, you mind stepping into my office? . . . Have a seat right there . . . Let me see. Hmm . . . Mister Mayhew, there's no reason to hold you any longer. You are free to go, but the front desk sergeant told me you are planning to sue?"

"I'm considering it."

"I can understand you are upset, but keep in mind the judge is more apt to side with the police. He knows them, but he doesn't know you from Adam. I suggest you let this go with my apology and return home to your wife. What's her name?"

"Ginny."

"Ginny? Not Ginny Mayhew . . . Oh my God. Cooper's girlfriend . . . !"

Klaus Gansel

I am Klaus Gansel and lucky enough to have some of my short stories published in the pages of FWA magazine and in two annual FWA collections. I'm still working on my memoir. For my next project I'll attempt to scale the dizzying heights of the Royal Palm Literary Awards.

The Pecking Order

"You are sixty-five years old. It is time to stop feeling guilty about causing World War II. You were not responsible for it."

"I didn't know that."

"Let us discus your guilt. Tell me about your childhood."

"The enemy bombed our street. My father was in the RAF. My mother couldn't have been a target—how can any one's mother be a target? So they must have been after me. I must have been very bad."

"You couldn't fight back. So you felt guilty."

"I did fight them. In *Kindergarten,* Nursery School, we didn't call it kindergarten then, I drew airplanes."

"Drew airplanes?"

"I could draw a Spitfire before I started school. I drew them fighting other planes—dog-fights."

"That was compulsive behavior. To resolve problems you needed more positive action."

"But my guys always won."

"Why did you draw airplanes?"

"There was a pecking order in nursery school. You were nothing if

17

you couldn't draw. Better drawers were higher peckers. If you learned to draw a new plane you jumped to the top."

"Pecker?"

"I could tell planes apart by the sound of their engines. I knew a Typhoon from a Focke Wolfe, a Hurricane from a Messerschmitt 109."

"Really!"

"Once, my friend was shot at by an enemy airplane. It was strafing the street. He recognized the sound of the engine and rolled under a hedge. For a while he was 'Top Pecker'."

"Hmm."

"I had a beautiful shrapnel collection. My best piece was about 6 inches long, sharp at both ends, from our back patio. Mum and I sometimes stood outside during a raid because our shelter was flooded and full of rats. If things got close, we hid under a mattress beneath the dining room table and Mum read Beatrix Potter to me."

"Read to you."

"Mum had just stepped back through the French doors when it hit the concrete right where she had been standing."

"It just missed your mother?"

"I think they were aiming for me."

"Did you take your collection to school?"

"No. Someone might have stolen it."

"Why did you collect shrapnel?"

"Souvenirs. We all collected shrapnel. It's something we did."

"More compulsive behavior."

"My best thing was an incendiary bomb. It hadn't gone off so I dragged it in from the street and hid it in the closet. Another one buried itself in the lawn but I couldn't dig it out. I scuffed over the hole it made so no one else could find it and have bragging rights. It's probably still there."

"What happened at the end of the war?"

"My father came home."

"How did you feel?"

"I was shy. I had never seen him before. Mum said he was the right man, but he looked like one of the soldiers who were billeted with us sometimes. I was scared to share secrets with him too soon so I waited before I showed him my bomb."

"Did he say anything?"

"Just, Jesus or something. I think he was jealous because he didn't bring anything like that back from the war."

"You left London after the war?"

"We moved to Africa. I couldn't find my bomb though. Maybe my dad gave it back—do you think?"

"Where in Africa?"

"Tanganyika, which once belonged to the Germans anyway. There was a swastika flag in our first house, and Dad made a big fuss of burning it because the enemy had dropped bombs on our house."

"The bombs you thought were aimed at you?"

"Yes. Mum and Dad sent me away to boarding school. Maybe they didn't feel safe with me around."

"Were you close to your parents?"

"I lived at boarding school mostly. After I graduated from high school I worked to get my air fare to go to college in Ireland. No English college would have me, but the Irish said it was no problem, they would kick me out if I was no good. They did. I think they knew about the war."

"Tell me more."

"Once all our windows were blown out by a bomb."

"How did you feel?"

"I forget."

"You are suppressing your feelings."

"I was thrown out of bed."

"So you *do* remember. It *was* close?"

"Of course it was close. They were all close. That's how I collected shrapnel and my incendiary bomb. To report the bomb damage we had to visit an office, on the top of a hill opposite a high school, and the sirens went off."

"Yes?"

"We heard the pockety-pockety noise of a Doodle Bug. Mum hugged me under a tree. It flew right over then its engine quit and it blew up about two miles away. There were workmen on the roof of the school, and they slid down their ladders to get to their air raid shelter."

"Go on."

"After a few years in Africa we came back to England and stayed with the family of a builder who was on that roof. He hurt his hands sliding down the ladder."

"You shouldn't read too much into that. It's just coincidence."

"That's easy for you to say. You've never been bombed, or sat under a table all night, or stood under a tree during an air-raid, or found a Swastika flag in your closet, or had your prize incendiary bomb stolen by your father. Or been sent away to school."

"Apart from your anger, let us consider the behavioral rut you have been in for the last sixty years."

"What do you mean?"

"You do the same thing over and over."

"Oh."

"It's compulsive."

"I've tried to figure it out. I sent for all sorts of stuff – tapes and visualization stuff—they promised to help with my life. My wife won't let me buy them anymore. She says they are frauds who want my money. But she was never bombed. And her ancestry is suspect. She says she's Irish, but she didn't tell me for several years after we were married, and I told you what they did to me! Anyway, her mother had far too many consonants in her name to be Irish!"

"If you keep repeating the same behavior it means you must be unhappy with proceeding forward."

"Why?"

"You have never resolved your own war."

"Really?"

"You must take positive action."

"I know how to resolve things. I told you. I did it by drawing. Oh, you mean get back at the enemy as an adult! Of course, bomb *them*. I know where one is. It's been in the lawn for 60 years. Now I know where I can use it, because I know where you come from, and why you ask all these questions. Trying to make *me* feel guilty for the war when it was probably your fault."

"You are trying to transfer blame. That is a good step. It means you recognize it."

"But is it really my guilt, or your guile! The word *guile*—that's Germanic. Dr. Miller. Ha! Think I was born yesterday, *Dr. Mueller?* Splash one enemy agent! Boy will I be the 'Top Pecker'."

"Yes, but you must first get out of this institution."

BOB HART

Bob Hart has written articles and stories for several publications including *The Florida Writer*, contributed to *FWA's Collection #1 - From Our Family to Yours, FWA Collection #2 - Slices of Life* and authored *Hart's Original Petpourri* (Langdon Street Press, 2010). His unpublished book, *Cageliners*, won second place in the 2010 RPLA Autobiography and Memoir category. (www.Originaldrhart.com)

A Dilemma

"I don't know if I can keep this a secret much longer."

"Have you any idea what will happen when we're found out?"

"I'm beyond caring. The sneaking around and…I'm sure I look guilty. We're gonna' get caught."

"You're just going to have to be strong! Look like you're in control. You're great at being the boss."

"I don't want to be strong. I just want to tell everyone how much I love you."

"I know, I truly do, but my family won't go along with this."

"But why? Wouldn't they be happy you'd found the love of your life, someone to grow old with, to be with till the end of time? I know I'm 10 years older than you, but…"

"Oh, that isn't it. To them, this isn't a good match. Nobody knows your background or family. Both those things are important to all my relatives. Mother refused to let my sister marry her fiancé because she didn't know his parents."

"That's nonsense! We are so lucky to have our lives together ahead of us. I don't want to waste a moment!"

"My sweetheart, my breath catches and my fingers tingle when you say that and ..."

"That's just how I felt when I first saw you. It was in the garden next to my home, where we both came for some peace and quiet, away from the blabberers at the cocktail party. Our eyes met and it was over for me."

"You looked handsome in your suit and tie – I love it when men get dressed up. You all look so glamorous."

"I'll not forget the dress you wore that matched your blue eyes. When I close my eyes now, I can see you looking over at me, slowly smiling, just teasing me to come get to know you."

"Why was it that it took a while for us to start to enjoy each other?"

"I didn't want to scare you away. I could have swept you up in my arms immediately. For once in my life, I behaved! 'Go slowly, boy,' I told myself."

"You behaved yourself? What does that mean? Maybe my family does have to worry about your past."

"My dear one, whatever you want to know, I'll tell you. Sometimes I don't think before I speak or act. Seeing you, I knew I had to use very proper manners. When something is perfect, you just don't want to mess up. That's how I feel."

"You know that makes me feel so treasured, don't you? Like nothing bad can ever happen to me."

"I can't believe I've found you. I want to take care of you forever."

"You know, maybe we can gather the clan this weekend and talk to them. If we can present our case thoroughly, we might be able to convince the family that our being together is a blessing. Let's make plans over dinner. Now, here's your cane. Can you push my wheelchair to the dining room?"

CAROLYN EVANS

Carolyn Evans regards raising her children her greatest accomplishment. She is a photographer, iconographer, was a children's theatre actor, and writes creative non-fiction. She has published one book and was a Top Ten Pick in *FWA's Collection #2 – Slices of Life*. She lives in Atlantic Beach, Florida.

Face Time

"Excuse me. Are you the girl doing Amy's makeup for homecoming?

"Yes, I'm Christina."

"I'm Adele, her mother. I hope you're good."

"Nice to meet you, Adele. Your daughter will be fine. I've been in the cosmetic industry for nine years."

"If she asks for Goth or something dramatic, don't listen to her. Just cover up her breakouts and keep her natural looking. Her dress is dark blue."

"But, Mom, I want my eyes dramatic."

"And I don't want you looking like a hooker. Like I said, don't listen to my daughter."

"How about pretty party makeup with good coverage? Have a seat, Amy. We have thirty minutes until my next appointment."

"Sit, Amy. Kristen needs all the time she can get with you."

"Oh, my name's Christina. It's easy to mix up with similar names."

"Yeah, okay. Listen, not too much eye liner."

"Mom, would you go? She has another appointment in thirty minutes."

"I'll keep the makeup classic, don't worry."

"Go, Mom!"

"See how kids are today? They're whiney, ungrateful, and have no respect for their parents."

"Do you have sensitive eyes or wear contacts, Amy?"

"No."

"Contacts? I should hope not. It's enough I have to buy expensive medicine for her problem skin. I wish you'd stop picking. Are you taking your pills? You better be. Tell her, Kristen. The medicine can't help her if she keeps tearing up her face."

"*Mom*, her name's Christina. Why don't you go get coffee?"

"This moisturizer is oil-free, Amy. It won't make you break out."

"Don't think I'm going to spend hundreds of dollars on your lotions and potions. Look at me—soap and water, and I have flawless skin. I don't know what happened to her. Must come from her father's side."

"Hold this mirror, and watch. I'm going to apply the foundation with a brush."

"Oh, brother, I need a coffee. I'll be back. And, Kristen, remember—*natural*."

"Thank God. Sorry about my mom. She's a trip."

"She just wants what's best for you. I bet you get good grades in school, don't you?"

"Yeah, how'd you know? I'm sure my Mom didn't tell you. She never tells people when I win a writing contest, get excellent marks at piano competitions, or make straight A's."

"Sounds like you're a super talented girl. What do you like better, writing or playing the piano?"

"I don't care about either."

"Really? Okay, how about this lip gloss color?"

"Yeah!"

"You know, Amy, your eyes light up when you smile. Smiling isn't such a bad habit to get into."

"According to Mom, I'm *all* bad habits."

"Uh-huh, but what do *you* think? How do *you* see yourself? I hope you don't sit in front of a magnifying mirror. Anyone can find flaws looking into those things. Have you tried busying your hands with something else? Sketching, baking—"

"It won't stop me. I wash my face and go to bed but can't sleep. So I get up and go to the bathroom and sit at the sink and pick."

"Do you have trouble sleeping *every* night?"

"Pretty much and I hate going to school, too."

"Time for shadow. Close your eyes, hon."

"Are you going to make them—"

"Gorgeous? Absolutely. You have beautiful eyes, and we'll enhance them for tonight."

"Uh, Christina?"

"Yes, Amy?"

"Thanks for being nice to me."

"Well, sure. I like you. Hey, who's the lucky guy you're going to homecoming with?"

"Nobody asked me. I'm going alone, like some other girls. But I'm riding with my friend, Jillian. She's my only friend really. She's a junior, too. Her dad's dropping us off at the auditorium. We planned tonight for weeks to make sure everything goes the way we decided."

"What are you talking about?"

"Jillian and I have a pact. She hates her life, too."

"A pact? You don't mean—"

"Hey, not too shabby, Kristen. You can't tell how bad her face is now."

"Oh, hi, Adele. Well, yes, you have a lovely daughter."

"Save your breath. You're not getting a tip. I'll buy a lipstick. That's it."

"You don't have to buy anything. Doing your daughter's makeup was my pleasure. But if you'd like a lipstick, they're on the other side of this bay, across from ladies fragrances. While you look, I'll finish up with Amy."

"Five minutes and we're leaving."

"No problem, Adele."

"Christina, will you please take a picture of me with my phone?"

"Sure. *Smile....* That was perfect. Can I get one of you with *my* phone?"

"If you want."

"Say *cheese sticks*. Excellent. I'd like to give you my cell number for future occasions, or, you know, if you have any questions about how I did your makeup today."

"It won't matter after tonight."

"Why, Amy? What about your prom in May? Oh, to be sixteen again. You have so much fun ahead of you."

"You say that because you're beautiful, Christina. You were probably never cut down by your mom, laughed at by boys, or snubbed by girls."

"Well, maybe moms don't change, but you'll be out of school before you know it."

"Then what? People are people. And most are mean."

"Put my number in your phone anyway. Here's my card."

"Fine."

"Good. Hey, Amy, did you notice my cuff? The stones are lapis lazuli. It's a bit wide, but I bet it'll go with your dress. So why don't you wear it tonight?"

"No, I—"

"Come on, take it off my wrist."

"All right. *Oh, my God—is* that a—"

"Scar? Yes."

"*You?* But, why?"

"In high school I wore glasses and was artsy. It wasn't until I was in college I discovered being artistic was cool. I had a great time. Not every day's perfect, but a lot of them are pretty awesome. I have my Aunt Marie to thank for all those days. Thirteen years ago, she showed up for me like a guardian angel, about a half hour after I'd.... Anyway, where's homecoming? I might want to stop by and see your dress."

"Really? You'd come to my dance?"

"If you promise I get to do your prom makeup in May."

"Well...."

"I insist on doing Jillian's, too."

"I guess Jillian and I can, uh, postpone our plans tonight till—"

"Good. And, hey, Amy, I love when you smile. Your eyes light up."

Cynthia Mallick

After an incarnation of teaching dance and choreographing, and another working as a makeup artist, the blank page I face now as a writer is familiar territory. Currently, I'm seeking representation for a young adult novel, while preparing other works to be published as e-books.

Character Assassination

"Hello."

"I've made my decision."

"Beth? It's two in the morning. What decision?"

"I've decided to get rid of George."

"What do you mean, get rid of?"

"Everything is getting too complicated. I need George out of the picture."

"Everyone likes George, have you thought of the consequences?"

"He won't be missed for long."

"What about Carol?"

"George is smothering her."

"But, is she strong enough to be on her own?"

"Not yet. She'll need a backbone."

"How can she get stronger if she has to deal with the loss of her husband?"

"Carol needs room to breathe. George has been overpowering her for too long."

"Are you sure, you want him out permanently?"

"Yes."

"You could have somebody rough him up, put him in the hospital with a coma or something."

"No, it has to be permanent."

"Okay, how will you do it?"

"I'm thinking about a car accident. Maybe cutting his brake lines before he leaves for his cabin in the Cascades."

"The police will suspect Carol."

"I'll make sure she has an alibi."

"It had better be fool proof. An abused wife is the first place they'll look."

"Believe me, she'll be seen as the victim she has become."

"Whom will you get to do it?"

"Remember several years ago when George was involved with that Ponzi scheme and managed to avoid prison time by turning states evidence against his financial advisor?"

"Sure, Bob the banker ended up taking the fall for everything. He's doing time in the state prison."

"It's been years, and Bob's been a model prisoner."

"You mean he's getting out early for good behavior."

"In addition, he's had lots of time to think about George's betrayal."

"Will he confront George or sneak up on him?"

"I'm so tired of George. I don't want him to have a chance to explain himself."

"How will it go down?"

"Bob knows about the cabin, he'll follow George out of town."

"How will he get to the brake lines?"

"George always stops at the same café just outside of Eaton for blackberry pie when it's in season."

"You want it done this summer?"

"Yes, the sooner the better."

"Are you going to let Bob get caught?"

"Maybe."

"Carol will make a very sympathetic character at the trial."

"That would be one way to look at it. However, it may be the perfect venue for her to gain her backbone when she addresses the defendant during the sentencing hearing."

"You have a point."

"I can see her going on to live an adventuresome life."

"So, you've made up your mind."

"Yes."

"As your editor, I can only make suggestions. It sounds like you have a great series in mind."

"Carol's story is going to be my next best-selling series."

"Goodnight, Beth."

"Goodnight, Martha. Sweet dreams."

MaryAnn Zahl

MaryAnn Zahl has moved over fifteen times in her forty years of marriage and currently resides in Tennessee. She enjoys traveling and has lived in three foreign countries. She considers writing a great stress reliever. She is married, has three children, and four (soon to be six) grandchildren.

Yes, Officer

"All right son, you know the drill. Spread 'em wide, hands on the cruiser."

"Yes, Officer."

"Anything in your pockets I need to know about?"

"No, Officer."

"What's this, a stuffed animal?"

"It's called a *Crazy Pug Bear*, a gift for my daughter, Officer."

"Is this what you stole from the toy store? Is this what they called the police about?"

"Yes, sir."

"You in the military son, what with the haircut, tattoo and all?"

"Yes, sir, the Marine Corps."

"Semper Fi, and all that, huh?"

"Yes, Officer."

"Are you stupid or something, son? You stealing this stuffed bear from the store is going to land you in jail. Damn, I've heard it all, now. Put your hands behind your back and don't you dare try anything, you hear?"

"Yes, sir."

"You have the right to remain silent. Anything you say can and will be used against you in a court of law. You have the right to speak to an attorney. If you cannot afford an attorney, one will be appointed for you. Do you understand these rights as they have been read to you?"

"Yes, Officer."

"Damn, can't you say anything other than, 'Yes Officer'?"

"Officer, you dropped something out of my wallet, there, there on the ground."

"This? Who is this pretty little thing?"

"That's my pride and joy officer, that's my Mattie, my little girl."

"Mattie? What kind of name is that?"

"It's short for Madeline, Officer. She was named after her grandmother."

"I'll hold onto your wallet until we get to the station. Watch your head son. Slide into the back of the cruiser."

"Yes, sir."

"Just settle in, we'll be back to the station in no time."

"Are you married, Officer?"

"No."

"Ever been in the service, Officer?"

"Yeah, sure was son, Navy. Saw lots of tattoos like yours. First I was assigned to Military Police then to the submarine *USS Cheyenne*, then back to MP duty in Subic Bay, Philippines."

"Boomer, huh?"

"Yeah, sailed the seven seas on a tiny, cramped, rollin' tincan, but loved every minute of it. But I really loved the Philippines."

"How long were you in for, Officer?"

"Eighteen years."

"God, you were almost a lifer. You had only two more years to go before retirement. Why did you get out so early?"

"I stopped getting letters from my wife and she would not answer my phone calls. I had friends check out the house and they said it was vacant. She skipped town with my kid."

"Damn, that hurts."

"Yeah, I tried getting Compassionate Leave to go find out what was going on, but no go. I jumped ship in Norfolk then spent two years hunting for her and her new boyfriend. Found them in Albuquerque,

New Mexico. She was working as a waitress and he was a mechanic. They were two of the sorriest losers you ever wanted to meet, but that kid of mine, she is like gold."

"What happened, Officer?"

"I went to take my little girl back home and they called the cops. Her mechanic buddy tried to stop me and I broke his jaw. I got arrested for assault. They let me go when they found out that they both had outstanding arrest warrants pending against them from three states for burglary and grand theft."

"What happened with the Navy?"

"My commanding officer went to bat for me and got me a discharge rather than being charged as a deserter. He helped me land this job here in my hometown with the Dallas Police Department. He saved my life and that of my little girl."

"Is that your little girl's picture on the dashboard, Officer?"

"Yeah, that's her, fifteen now, she's a heartbreaker. It bugs her because I want to meet all of her dates before they take her out. The boys freak out when they see the police car in the driveway. But deep down inside she loves it that I care so much."

"Yes, Officer. I remember this neighborhood growin' up as a kid here. That was before it was taken over by all of the gangs and before I went into the Marine Corps. Neighborhood sure has changed. My house is just down this road."

"You grew up here?"

"Yes, sir, before I went into the Marine Corps."

"Why did you come back?"

"My wife died six months ago of an overdose and I used all the money that I had in the bank to get back here and get my little girl. I got Compassionate Leave from the Marines to come home for my daughter's birthday. I wanted to get her a birthday present but I ran out of money. I don't know how I will pay for the ticket back to California when I get out of jail and report back for duty."

"What about your little girl?"

"My sister is going to take care of her for the next six months until I get out of the Marine Corps. I already have a job lined up at Akers Hardware as an Assistant Manager or at least I did have a job lined up."

"What do you mean?"

"They don't hire anyone with a criminal record."

"We'll be at the station soon. You know I have to take you in son, don't you?

"Yes, officer. I understand, you are just doing your duty. Just like we all have to, we all have to do our duty."

"Is that why you stole that teddy bear, for your daughter's birthday?"

"Yes, Officer. I have disappointed her so many times before I did not want to disappoint her again, ever."

"How much was that bear, son?"

"It was thirty-nine dollars, Officer."

"You risked your freedom for thirty-nine dollars?"

"Yes, sir, but I have risked my life for a hell of a lot less, sir."

"I understand but wait just a moment. Over fifty-dollars is a felony, under fifty is a misdemeanor. Hold on son, I am pulling the car over. That bear cost less than fifty-dollars and therefore its up to the discretion of the responding officer. I am going to see that the store gets the money for the bear and you get home to your little girl, do you hear me?"

"But Officer, I don't have the money to pay for the bear."

"I know that, dimwit. You already paid for it overseas and don't even realize it. Here, take the bear and I better not ever catch you stealing around here again, you understand me? I'll square it with the store. Now git. Here's your wallet back with the picture of your little girl."

"Officer, this wallet has three-hundred dollars in it."

"Are you saying there was more money in before?"

"No, my wallet was empty when I gave it to you officer. I had no…"

"I told you git, now. I mean it, before I change my mind."

"Yes, Officer. Thank you."

"No, thank you, son. Say Happy Birthday to your little girl for me."

"Yes, Officer."

Bryan Mooney

Bryan Mooney is a prolific writer, originally from the Midwest before being lured to the tropical warmth of the East Coast where he lives with his longtime wife, Bonnie. He enjoys penning contemporary romance but his true passion is writing stories that have an impact on peoples' lives.

Troubled Water

"What the hell are you doing here?"

"You asked me to come, remember?"

"You weren't there my whole life, why now?"

"Because you asked."

"Oh, just like that eh? Just ask and my dad pops up out of the grave. Why didn't you do something like this when it actually mattered?"

"Son, I wasn't a good father. There's no disputing that. But I have an opportunity to make amends, however small they may be."

" 'Son'. There's a laugh. When was I ever your son? Dads go to their son's basketball games. Dads teach sons how to fix things. Dads guide sons to be good fathers. I was nothing but an inconvenience to you."

"What can I say? 'I'm sorry' fills my soul with the word inadequate. 'Please forgive me' drowns in the feeling of too-little-too-late. I have no capacity to make anything up to you other than being here for you right here, right now."

"Remember when I was riding on the handlebars of that bike with you? I was only about six-years-old. I accidentally stuck my foot in the spokes and sent us both tumbling. I remember you flew over my head.

I couldn't walk well for days. You got mad at me. That fucking sucked."

"I was scared. I didn't know whether you were hurt bad or what. I didn't know how to show compassion."

"That's for damn sure. I got laughed at for riding that oversized rickety bike when all the other kids had those cool 'banana seat' bikes. Their bikes looked like Ferraris. Mine looked like an old semi."

"I squandered money on women and booze. What little remained we needed for food and shelter."

"What is this? Honesty? Now? I needed this about fifty years ago. You're not telling me anything I didn't already know."

"True, but it's not something you ever heard from me. Honesty came hard for me. I always felt like owning up to my shortcomings would make me appear weak. The fact is my lies damaged the people I love."

"Love? There's another good one. Since you're being so up front and honest, did you ever love anyone other than yourself?"

"I know how it looked. A dozen women on the side. Me drinking myself blind on holidays, days off or any other occasion I could justify a swig or ten. I know I appeared selfish. In fact, I was selfish. But it wasn't out of a love of myself. I hated who I was. I loved my family – your mom, your sisters and you."

"Bullshit. I'm your only son. I only remember two times in my life where you spent time with me one-on-one. The bicycle incident is one, and I only remember the wreck. Basketball at the Police Lodge is the other. Remember that?"

"Yes."

"Why are you smiling? Your lack of attention back then was pathetic."

"I'm smiling because that hour we spent shooting hoops is one of the few times I truly felt like a father."

"Why the hell didn't you do more of it then? I made the school basketball team. I was scared. I didn't know how to act around all those athletes. I felt out of place. Unsure of myself. I beat out a couple dozen other players to make the team but I rode the bench and felt worthless. You didn't come to a single game."

"Like I said. I damaged those I love. In your case, I crippled you emotionally."

"What the fuck is that supposed to mean? I've handled myself extremely well throughout my life. I'm people skilled, I know how to relate to others and I can motivate people."

"Yes, but you can't take care of yourself. Look where you're at right now."

"What do you know about this? You never cared enough to reach out to anyone. Life was all about you. Your sex drive. Your Old Crow. Your karaoke. You, you, you."

"Guilty. On all counts. I feared reaching out. Reaching out meant weakness. It meant I had to show a soft side. My view of manhood said soft meant I was a panty-waist. I admire the man you have become. You are everything I wanted to be but couldn't seem to achieve."

"All I wanted was my dad. I was raised by a mom and three sisters. What do they know about being a man?"

"They did a pretty good job under the circumstances."

"I never learned how to fight. How to stand up for myself. I never learned how to stare down a bully. Sure, I learned diplomacy, but I also learned how to run."

"Be honest son. Were any of those potential fights worth a beating? What you learned was to walk away. I never learned that lesson."

"At the time, yes. At least I wouldn't have always felt worthless. The closest I ever came to a fight, my best friend J.B. whipped Mark Thomas' ass. Another instance where I lost self-esteem. I couldn't even fight my own fights."

"Son, this isn't about fights or lack of fights, or your mom or your sisters. You're here because I failed to be a father to you. Can't we find a way to step back, literally and figuratively, and work through some of this?"

"What do you care?"

"I'm here."

"Yeah. Great. That again."

"Son, could you ever forgive me?"

"Why should I?"

"Until you forgive me, you can't forgive yourself."

"Oh. Great. Now you're turning psychologist on me?"

"No. I'm simply stating the truth. You're here on this bridge because you feel the oppressive weight of perceived failure. Much of the worthlessness you feel falls on my shoulders. I let you down. But I still love you. My hope is that some part of you can let go of the pain I caused and find a way to forgive."

"There are no happy endings here. You're dead. I'm about to be. End of story."

"The pain remains. You're not escaping anything. Don't make my mistake."

"Your mistake? You died of old age. Your sorry, miserable, negative-assed self lived to be ninety and you died in your sleep. How am I making your mistake?"

"I died without my family knowing how much I love them. I distanced myself. Yes, miserable, negative-assed and all. You do this and your wife and children will question why and whether you really loved them."

"Leave them out of this."

"I can't. I know you love them. What you're doing is selfish, just like I was. Don't make my mistake. Reach down deep, find some forgiveness and go love your family."

"You're a bastard."

"Right now I'm your dad and I plead for your forgiveness. I don't deserve it, but isn't that the nature of forgiveness? Isn't it for those who don't deserve it?"

"I suppose, but I don't know if I can do it."

"Isn't the doubt enough to make you step back and consider it?"

"I do love my family. You knew I wouldn't jump, didn't you?"

"No, actually I feared you would."

"I wish I could have known you like this when you were alive."

"Me too, son. Me too."

Michael Ray King

Michael Ray King has authored three books, won five RPLA's and co-leads the Palm Coast Chapter of FWA. Michael is the President of ClearView Press Inc., President of Palm Coast's local Toastmasters club and founder of the Rogues Gallery Writers - a small, focus writing group. www.michaelrayking.com

Extermination

"IT'S TIME WE DID SOMETHING ABOUT THESE HUMANS!"

"You don't have to shout; I can hear you perfectly well at normal tones."

"I ALWAYS TALK LIKE THIS."

"How about trying it at a whisper?"

"Very well. Now, as I was saying …"

"Yes, yes, the humans. You've had a love/hate relationship with them ever since you created them. This won't be the first time you've tried getting rid of them."

"I never should have taken pity on Noah. I could have squashed the species right then."

"Your problem is you're fascinated with mankind. I can't count how many times you've commented on how amazing they are."

"True, true. I remember the first time one of them figured out how to use fire, I nearly dropped my scepter. From there, creating the wheel, and then writing, and now … the aeroplane! I still can't believe those things ever get off the ground."

"So what's got your robes itchy this time? Some of those atheists piss you off again?"

"Now Gabe, do you really think I'd try to kill off the whole species over a few inappropriate religious beliefs? You think I'm that vengeful?"

"Can you say Sodom and Gomorrah?"

"You always bring them up."

"All I can say is we angels thought it hilarious when you turned Lot's wife into salt. You should've seen Thamma's face! What a scream."

"I've had my moments, I admit it. It used to be I could knock off a city or two and people would turn back to their righteous ways. But, as they say, that's history."

"So why IS it you want to kill off all *homo sapiens*?"

"Just look at what they're doing to the planet! Nuclear bombs, forest devastation, global warming … in another hundred years, all that'll be left will be barren rocks and empty seas."

"Sounds like your problem will solve itself?"

"I don't want EVERYTHING destroyed – took too long to build it up this far. Don't forget that ongoing contest with the God over in Alpha Centauri about creating the highest life form. He held the lead with some interesting mosses and lichens, but ever since I created insects I've been going full steam. Gotta love those insects."

"You should be alright then. I think the cockroach is going to survive no matter what kind of mess the humans make."

"ROFL as the cherubs like to say, dear Gabe, ROFL. You know what that means?"

"Yeah, boss. Don't try to be hip. It's undignified."

"I'm God. I can do anything I want."

"Okay, so back to this human thing. What are your plans for doing them in? Not disease again, I hope. The plague worked pretty well in the middle ages, but with all their modern medicine the HIV hasn't made a dent."

"You have to admit it slowed down infidelity."

"Not much."

"Agreed."

"So what are you thinking this time? We're all eager to hear the newest and greatest from Mr. Omnipotent."

"It's a two shot deal. I start with natural disasters; hurricanes, earthquakes, floods, drought … that kind of thing. The human really is a weak creature, you know. If he loses all his tools and nearly starves, he'll degenerate into the hairless ape from which he came."

"I'm with you so far – though from what I've seen, even if only a small band of them are left, they procreate so quickly they'll bounce right back. You're not thinking of replacing them with the big and gentle creature again? Neither the whale nor the mammoth stood a chance against the hominids."

"Nope, more severe than that. Remember how I took out the dinosaurs?"

"You planning on another huge meteor in the desert that'll blot out the sun for a few hundred years?"

"Something like that, but a little quicker. After the earthquakes, a little flash play, courtesy of a big sun flare. I'll give the earth a light surface scorch, just enough to kill off the higher species, and start over from the insects and mollusks. Build up from the invertebrates again. In a quarter million years I should have something pretty good."

"Shake and bake, huh? Great idea. I'll notify the other angels and we'll bring marshmallows."

PHILIP L. LEVIN

Philip Levin serves as president of the Gulf Coast Writers Association in Mississippi. His published works include the mystery "Inheritance," children's photo books "Consuto" and "Ndovu," and editor of the "Afternoon Tales" anthology series. His "Andrew Comes Home" won an RWA grand prize. His favorite vacation spot is Kenya.

Big Fish

"It's been years since I've been in your office, Jack. Last time was after Columbia, wasn't it?"

"I guess so. Sit down. You're making me nervous. Screw formality. We've known each other for thirty years."

"Thirty-two."

"There you go again."

"I'm an engineer. If they had listened to the engineers instead of the managers we'd still have the Challenger and Columbia in the fleet."

"You're preaching to the choir. How's Mazie?"

"Nervous."

"The girls?"

"We don't tell them anything. They're busy with college—boys. You know. Why am I here?"

"You know why."

"Yeah. I guess I do, don't I. Did you tell them I have twenty-eight years? Two more and I get a pension. They're keeping a skeleton crew, aren't they, for God's sake? Why put me out? I've got more knowledge of the program in my little finger than these new kids have in their whole overblown brains. I can still contribute, Jack. Let me talk to them."

"You don't think I've told them that? You make too much money. Why would they pay you a hundred grand to sit on your ass waiting for another contract when they can keep a kid a year out of college for sixty, and the kid's got a good ticker and a flat belly? We're dinosaurs, Paul. Big, expensive, fat dinosaurs and we're at the mercy of whoever the hell's president. If he had a vision like Kennedy, then we could show the world what Americans are made of. But if the guy doesn't have a clue about the space program then he's going to dump it and us with it."

"By us, you mean me."

"Yeah, you, and six thousand others just like you. It'll take us ten years to gain back the knowledge we're throwing out in one month. Shortsighted, money- hungry politicians. I swear to God, if these clowns had been in charge during World War Two, we'd be speaking German."

"Don't hold back, Jack. Tell me how you really feel."

"I'm upset and I want to kick something. That's how I feel."

"I'm the one losing my job."

"Sorry, Paul. I really am. If there was anything I could have done, I would. You know that. They won't even kick in for a severance. You've got a month until Atlantis and then a couple of days to clear out your desk. Listen, some of the union techs and electricians have set up a gig in an orange processing plant in Lakeland. Two months work at twenty-five an hour, but you'll have to do some wire pulling and check-out. I signed you up. In a way, it's like a severance until you find work. How's that sound?"

"No one's going to hire me, Jack. I'm fifty-five with existing health issues as baggage. It's over. It's been a nice ride and I had a good time, but it's over."

"What the hell are you talking about? Don't do anything stupid."

"There's nothing stupid about it. If I expire on the premises, then my life equates to four hundred, thirty-six thousand, and ten dollars. Enough to take care of Mazie, enough to keep the house, enough to get the girls through college. If it happens off base, I'm not worth a pot to piss in."

"All right. Stop it. If I even think you're going to do something like that, I'll call security and have them escort you out on your ass. Who the hell am I going to play golf with if you're gone? Now cut it out, okay? You're not the only guy in the world to lose a job. Sometimes it's for the better. Somebody will pick you up and maybe it'll be a start-up, high tech, or something. In five years, you could buy what's left of the space program. No more nonsense, I'm serious."

"I'm not giving you a choice, Jack. I've made up my mind. What I'm asking is for you to do me this last favor as a friend. I want you to lie, to cover it up, to tell the press, yeah, Paul was upbeat, ready for a new challenge. Tell them, you're sure it was an accident. Paul was the last guy in the world to take his own life. I'm asking—I'm begging you to do this for me as a friend."

"I can't."

"Why not?"

"You're like a brother. I'm not going to be responsible—."

"I'll be responsible, not you. It's my decision and it's the right one—the only one."

"And what about Mazie and the girls? They'll never get over it. You're more important to them than a house or college. Ask them."

"They'll get over it."

"How do you know that? What are you, God?"

"I said—they'll get over it. Everyone does eventually. I lost my brother twenty years ago. At first, I was devastated. I prayed to God for it to be a mistake. Bring him back, he was too young. For a year, I'd stop by the cemetery each month to talk, to clean the marker, to dust the cheap plastic flowers, but it didn't last. Now I only visit on his birthday. I can't even remember what he looked like unless I pull out a picture. You forget. You go on with your life. It will be rough on the girls and Mazie for a while, but they'll get over it. They'll move on. People do that. They always have and they always will. I'm going through with it, Jack, and I don't want you to stop me. I want your word. The word as a friend. The word as a blood brother. We made a pact and I want you to keep it."

"That was thirty years ago. We were stupid."

"Thirty-two, and it was the greatest fishing trip we ever took. New hires, money to burn, single, the Costa Rican sun, and Costa Rican girls."

"I still have a scar on my thumb, but you can barely see it. If you had sharpened your knife it would have healed better."

"Yeah, and if you hadn't been a coward you would have cut your own damn thumb. But we did it and when we shared blood I took it seriously and I want you to do the same. So what about it?"

"Yeah—so what about it."

"Remember the fish? The big one?"

"I remember."

"The mate called you a little girl and took the rod from you."

"It was big, I couldn't handle it."

"He landed it without a sweat."

"It was a big fish."

"Big damn fish."

"Yeah—big fish."

JOHN J. WHITE

John J. White has had stories and articles published in anthologies and magazines around the world. He has won awards for his novels and short fiction, including honors from the Alabama Writers Conclave, Writers-Editors International, Maryland Writers and Writer's Digest. He lives in Merritt Island, Florida with his wife, Pamela. www.jjwhite.org

Feng Shui

"Ruth, what is going on in here? Baking a turkey in the middle of the week?"

"Shh, Howard! You'll disturb her. She's smudging."

"Disturb who? Who's this she? Smudging what?"

"Her name's Maxine. She's cleansing the negative energy. She's in the back of the house."

"Why's she taking a bath in the back of our house?"

"Not a bath. Cleansing. Clearing. It's part of the ceremony."

"Where's our furniture? The sofa? And where's my chair?"

"Your chair was blocking the chi."

"What the hell's shee?"

"Chi not she. And please, keep your voice down. Our bagua was all wrong. It's a wonder the chi moved at all in this house."

"Bag-what?"

"Bagua, Howard."

"Is this a joke? That's it. A practical joke. Good one. Now tell your friend in the back it worked and she can go home. That smell's making me hungry. And where'd you hide my chair?"

"I turned it back to the universe. Don't you feel the freshness and freedom? Just look at this room. Maxine hasn't even cleansed it yet and I feel a fantastic energy in here."

"Have you lost your mind?"

"Not at all. And the energy's thanking us."

"Oh. My. God. Where's the television? What are those pillows for?"

"You sit on them. And you don't need TV. Maxine says that channels negative energy."

"232 channels to be precise. Where is my T.V?"

"In the garage. I'm putting it on Craig's list."

"The hell you say."

"Not so loud. Come on, sit down here with me. Isn't this a nice conversation area? Or we could meditate."

"I can't get down there. I'm sixty-three years old for Chrissakes. I'll never get back up."

"They sit on cushions in China and Japan."

"I don't care about China and Japan. This is Orlando. I sit on a chair. And what's all that foofoo over there?"

"That's the love and marriage corner. Maxine says candles and flowers represent love. I didn't have any ducks so I put those two cat figurines there. I'm going to look for a pair of ducks. Or maybe cranes. They mate for life Maxine says—"

"Maxine, Maxine. Maxine says to jump into a burning fire, you going to do it?"

"Shh! Here she comes. Help me up."

"Give me your hand. On the count of three."

"You didn't have to yank me up that hard and you didn't even count to three."

"She isn't much of a talker."

"She's focused on the cleansing."

"Does she have to keep banging that gong?"

"You don't have to talk about her like she can't hear."

"Don't mind me. I just live here. Hey, she banged that thing right in my ear."

"You're in the spot she needed to cleanse. Did you feel that energy wave?"

"She did that on purpose, I know she did. Banged that damn thing next to my ear."

"It's a sacred gong. Now she needs to smudge us."

"You're kidding. At least she's stopped clanging that thing."

"Maxine says the smoke follows the chi."

"Give me a break. Hey, get that smoky thing away from me."

"Stand still. She's cleansing our aura with the smoke from the sage. Then she sprinkles salt."

"This is insane. It smells like Thanksgiving dinner in here. And who cleans up all that salt?"

"It stays there."

"Stays there? You need to see your endocrinologist, Ruth. Your thyroid's out of whack again."

"It is not! We need to turn loose of things that don't serve us so we can focus on what's important."

"Focus on what? I just want to sit in my chair and watch a Braves game. Is that too much to ask?"

"We don't have that many more years."

"What's that got to do with the salt shaker lady here?"

"Humor me. This is important to me. To us."

"Just like yoga was important. Then your Tai Chi and then those angel classes. All those came and went. This one stepped a little over the line."

"You mean because I took your chair?"

"And the TV."

"I think she's done."

"How much do we owe her?"

"I paid her already."

"So how about dinner?"

"How about vegetarian?"

"How about burgers and beer?"

"Let me fix my makeup."

"You look just fine just like you are."

"I love you, Howard."

"And I love you, Ruth. Whatever this chee-thing is, you've moved mine for thirty-eight years. Now if we hurry, we can get a table by the big screen."

"Who's pitching?"

"Who cares?"

KAREN BLONDEAU

Karen Blondeau writes. She's filled countless spiral notebooks, leather bound journals and electronic flash drives with short stories, flash fiction, poetry and novellas. Her work has been published in anthologies, including *FWA Collection #2 - Slices of Life*, and won contests. A passion for passion, her favorite writing genre is contemporary romance. Karen lives in Central Florida with her ever-patient husband, Mike.

The Wanderer

"It's early . . . isn't it?"

"What? I didn't see you!"

"I didn't mean to scare you, ma'am. I know I don't look so great. I been travelin' all night long."

"What do you want?"

"Well, ma'am, I'm new in town, y'know? Don't know a soul. You work in this building?"

"Why do you want to know?"

"Someone down the street said that *Melody Musicals* might be in here."

"I'm not sure. The building's not open yet, so come back later and look around. It's not a large building."

"Oh, you have a key. I'll just go in with you and try to find them. Are you all by yourself?"

"No! Come back in about thirty minutes. My boss is waiting for me. I have to go."

"Ma'am, I'm Ray Dixon. I want to make it big in country music. At home, I heard that *Melody Musicals* can help me get ready to go to Nashville, where folks like me have a chance, y'know? I think they'll like me."

"I hope they do, but I'll leave you now, Mr. Dixon. You should come back when stores are opening."

"It's okay, ma'am . . . I'll get the door for you. You go ahead in."

◆

"Well, it's sure gloomy in here, but the sun'll be shinin' in any minute now,

don't you think?"

"I hope so. Please, Mr. Dixon! Please wait over there. Goodbye."

"You're goin' upstairs?"

"Yes. Our office is at the top of the stairs. My boss is waiting."

"I don't see no lights up there, ma'am. I guess your boss ain't here yet, so I'll go up with you."

"No! He'll be here any minute."

"Ma'am, don't worry. I won't take much of your time. Like I said, I'm new in town and . . ."

"Look, Mr. Dixon. The sun is beginning to shine through the skylight, so the other stores should be opening soon. Maybe you can look around now."

"Okay. But I'd appreciate it if you call me 'Ray.'"

◆

"Ma'am, ma'am! I need to ask you somethin', but your door's locked. Can you hear me through the glass? Isn't your boss here yet?"

"He called . . . he's on his way, so I guess you can come on in. What do you need? Didn't you find *Melody Musicals?*"

"Yeah, I did, but they're not the ones. The guy there said I need to talk to the folks at *New Country Artists.* Can you tell me how to get there?"

"Couldn't he tell you?"

"No, he's sorta new in town too, y'know, so he ain't sure how to get there, but he said it's in another part of town."

"All right, Ray. What's their address?"

"Here's what he put down for me."

"Yes, I know the area. I'll write directions for you."

"I want to thank you, ma'am. You know, when I got in town I was just wanderin' around. I didn't know a soul, and then you showed up out of the blue. You've sure been a good friend."

"I'm glad I could help. Good luck!"

"You're gonna hear about me before long in country music, ma'am. Don't forget my name."

"Oh, I won't forget. I won't forget Ray Dixon."

JOYCE BOWDEN

Joyce Bowden, a free-lance editor, lives in Orlando. She thinks of herself as a *neoteric* woman (up-to-date and modern), a trait she instilled in her four daughters and shares with her fiance. Her memoir *Number One Sun* describes her pride to be descended from original settlers in Kentucky in 1787.

Gotta Play to Win

"I've changed my mind."

"But Doris, we drove nearly two hours to get here. We can't just get in the car and go home. Come on, it'll be fun."

"Looky here. This was your idea, not mine. I was content to stay at home. But no. Shirley had bigger plans for me. Said I needed to get outta the house."

"And you do. You've been cooped up there since Harry died. He'd want you to go out and have some fun. Remember how much he loved this place? All the noises–the hooting and howling and bells? And you agreed last week that you'd do this. Now come on."

"Maybe I can get a ride home on one of them buses that bring people to the casino."

"You're not going home. And that's final."

"Okay, Shirley. But I don't wanna stay long."

"Listen to all the noise, Doris. Doesn't it give you goose bumps? Maybe we'll be big winners. Think of what we could buy with our winnings. Did Harry have a favorite slot machine? You can play that one."

"Brrr, and pooey. It's freezin' and stinks in here."

"That's why I had you bring a sweater, Doris. We'll head to the bigger room where it's not so smoky. Now come on."

"Just don't leave me alone. Don't go wanderin' off all over the place."

"I won't. You pick out a machine and I'll play the one next to it."

"Harry liked the poker slots. Don't know which one."

"Then we'll find some poker machines to play. But first off, we need to get you signed up for a card so you can get points when you play. The sign-up desk is in the big room. There are lots more slots in there, too."

"What I need a card for, Shirley?"

"You stick it in the machine and earn points every time you play—whether you win or lose. You use the points to buy stuff in here, or for lunch. And they'll send you packets each month with coupons for meals and free playing money. They have drawings every week for big prizes. The card registers you for the drawings. Today, you could win a Harley. "

"Now, what the heck would I want a motorcycle for? I'm lucky to be able to drive my golf cart. I'd kill myself on a bike."

"Chances are you won't win it anyway. But I guess if you do, you could sell it. Harley's are supposed to be top of the line. I'll bet you could get a bunch for it."

"Or we could just leave your car here, and ride it home."

"That's the spirit, Doris."

"Yeah, couldn't you just see the two of us as motorcycle mommas? Wind whippin' our hair. Bugs gettin' in our teeth. But we'd have to stop on the way to get tattoos. Can't ride a bike without a proper tattoo."

"Keep dreaming, girl. Now, let's find those poker machines."

"Here's two side-by-side. I'll take this one."

"What are you doing, Doris? You gotta bet the maximum to win anything."

"But that's a dollar and a quarter every time I hit the button. Maybe I should play one of them penny machines we passed."

"For Pete's sake. I swear you can squeeze a nickel so hard the Indian's riding the buffalo. Harry left you plenty. I can just hear him now. 'Doris,' he'd say. 'Now don't be cheap, honey. It's my money. Spend it like I would. Go for the big win.'"

"He did like it here, didn't he?"

"As Sarah Palin would say, 'You betcha.' Now let go of that cash."

"Okay, I'll bet the max ... Hey, what's that I got?"

"It's a full house. See? Look at how much you won on one pull."

"Well, that was lucky. But now it's startin' to suck up my winnin's."

"Just keep playing, Doris ... Holy cow! You just got four of a kind."

"Woo-eee! This is fun. Now I see why Harry liked it so much. Come on, baby. Momma needs a new pair of shoes. Well, drat. The thing is takin' away my money again. Hey Shirley, why are them people rubbin' the screens like that?"

"They think it'll bring them luck. I think it just spreads germs. But maybe I'll give it a try, since I don't seem to be getting much of anything here."

"What's that announcer sayin'?"

"He's getting ready to call a name for the big prize. They have a drawing every hour."

"Let's listen careful then ... Was that my name he just called?"

"It was, Doris. Let's cash out of these machines and get up there."

"Don't run so fast. My short legs don't move like yours."

"Yoo, hoo! Here she is! Now Doris, get up on the stage and show him your ID. Good luck, girl."

"So I gotta spin this wheel to see what I won? Okay then. Here goes."

"Go, Doris! Go, Doris! Come on everybody. Go, Doris!"

"Holy jamoly! It landed on five thousand. Is that what I win? Do I hafta spend it here? Look, Shirley! I won a buncha money!"

"I can't believe you won so much. Harry would be so proud. And you wanted to go back home. What do you think now?"

"Since I guess I'm on a winnin' streak, there's just one thing to do."

"What's that?"

"Let's spend the night."

Susan Boyd

Susan Boyd retired from the Bureau of Alcohol, Tobacco, Firearms and Explosives (ATF) in 2007. Pursuing her literary interests in retirement, she has written several award-winning short stories, and one novel. Susan is an avid pickleball player, golfer, bridge player, and bowler. She resides in The Villages, Florida with her husband, Larry.

Sightseeing

"Today our scenic voyage has taken us along the picturesque seaside and resorts of the Gulf coast, and now onto St. Pete Beach, one of the finest shorelines of North America and the final leg of our journey today. I hope you're enjoying the tour so far."

"Yes. It's been delightful, along with the colorful language used to describe other drivers."

"Uh...yes...well...as I was saying, we're progressing along one of the most relaxing vacation resort destinations, perfect for a romantic honeymoon or any special affair, like yours...a rather important event."

"Yes, yes...celebrating forty-five years of marriage...and we couldn't be happier."

"That's truly something to treasure...Congratulations. You certainly have reason to celebrate."

"Why, thank you kind sir. Yes, I expect we'll enjoy many more fun filled years together."

"Wonderful news...and might I say, you chose the perfect place to commemorate such a momentous occasion...and the perfect guide. I offer only the very best private tours, and hope this will be one you'll cherish."

"I'm sure it will be. Every minute so far has been spectacular. You know, I've never been to Florida. Traveling has always been beyond our means…you really have no idea what this means to me."

"Ah yes, I can well imagine, and fully appreciate your enthusiasm. As a retired veteran, I've travelled the world and seen a lot of places, but none so relaxing and intoxicating as the sweet air and white sands of St. Petersburg."

"Mmmm…breathtaking, I want to take it all in."

"Then I shall do my best to accommodate…Now coming up on our left, we have the small, brightly painted stores and restaurants of St. Pete Beach's shopping district. Here is Florida in all its passion with numerous bistros and boutiques decked out in the traditional coral-pink, ocean-blue, and citrus-yellow. These shops are crammed with trinkets and baubles to delight the hearts and bleed the wallets of many a visitor. And it's a beautiful day to enjoy our drive. It appears that all the locals and tourists are enjoying it as well, all out in full force today. People meandering across the street are forcing us to slow to a crawl. So, let's take advantage of this opportunity to view the coastline. To our right we're offered an even greater taste of the area. Endless beach-side pubs and tiki bars are brimming with tanned and burned bodies. There are beachgoers in bikinis and speedos everywhere…providing some things worth seeing…and others…well, not so much."

"Huh…how amusing…and delightful."

"Yes it is. And here…coming up on our right…the exquisite "Pink Palace" known as the Don Cesar. One of the grandest five star resorts in Florida. This lavish building, constructed in 1928, is listed on the National Register of Historic Places and exhibits a blending of Moorish and Mediterranean architecture, fitting well with the Spanish Colonial styling of St. Petersburg. It boasts numerous elaborate suites and seaside views, and a top of the line spa for its diverse and privileged clientele."

"I understand presidents and royalty have stayed here?"

"Yes. Many a famous comedian, rock star, and aristocrat have graced the luxurious accommodations of this hotel, along with several presidents, including Franklin D. Roosevelt…"

"Wow, it really is something…isn't it Harry?"

"…And it sits upon snow white sands. I will pull over shortly so you may appreciate the Gulf in all its glory. Ah…and here we go, rounding out our circuit today, we've saved the best for last. Before us now are pallid, powder sands caressed by aquamarine waves, lapping ashore as a brilliant sun glistens and dances across the water's surface. This is a choice spot for sailing, jet-skiing, parasailing, and windsurfing. It's also a prime location for sunning, swimming, and shelling…if the beach is your thing."

"Believe me, it is. I can almost hear the waves crashing onto the shoreline from here."

"Take a moment, sit back and relax, drink it all in…the opulence of the soothing ocean and soft sands."

"Harry, it's wonderful!"

"I wish we could remain longer my dear lady, so you might walk the shoreline and dip your toes into the warm waves, but unfortunately time does not permit…"

"—Oh no…please, don't feel badly. That's a pleasure we'll save for another day."

"Indeed. I hope you'll soon have the opportunity to enjoy what I can now only provide at a glimpse."

"Honestly, I think sightseeing is as much fun as playing in the sun. At least this way my husband and I won't get sunburned."

"True madam…"

"Besides, your tour provides so much…I can nearly feel the sea breeze rippling over my skin and hear the gulls squawking from here. It's like I'm right there…on the beach…the smell of salty ocean air surrounding me, blowing fine sand into my face and hair. Oh…how enchanting it all is. And the water…is it warm or cool?"

"The water is refreshing this time of year…quite warm along the shoreline but much cooler further out into the Gulf. And way out, as far as the eye can see, are white caps that rise and roll, slowly making their way onto shore. Ah…and further out still—beyond the boaters and swimmers—are dolphins rising and cresting the water's surface. In the blink of an eye, they plunge back in and disappear again. But all good things must end, and it is here that our tour draws to a close. Sadly, my dear lady, our voyage has concluded."

"The engine stopped. Harry, don't tell me it's over so soon. Are we home already?"

"Yes, Emma…my dear, I'm afraid so."

"Aw, our drives go by too quickly."

"But did you enjoy your vacation day my dear?"

"Oh yes, as always. Harold, you are a perfect gentleman and gracious host. Without a doubt, my favorite tour guide…and the best husband a woman could ever wish for."

"Happy Anniversary my dear."

"Happy Anniversary Harry…I love you."

"I love you too Emma. I only wish I could provide the real thing. You deserve it."

"Well, I prefer our sightseeing trips. They're always fun and entertaining…besides; you know I can't tell the difference. Your descriptive tours are more revealing for me than traveling to a destination I cannot see anyway. So, it really doesn't matter where we go…even if we're only cruising around the block, so long as we're together…that's all that matters to me."

"Well then my dear, you shall have what you desire…and the world awaits you. Where shall we go tomorrow…the Swiss Alps perhaps, maybe Yellowstone Park, or the Grand Canyon?"

"No, how about some place more romantic, more Mediterranean …how about Italy? I'd love to see Venice…and Rome…and then maybe Greece, if we have time."

"You've got it my dear. Tomorrow we shall tour Italy…and continue on from there. And with a loving guide by your side…you, my dear Emma, shall see the world."

CATE BRONSON

Cate Bronson is a freelance writer working on a fiction thriller, science-fiction trilogy, and nonfiction book. She has had several fiction stories published and been awarded recognition by Writer's Digest for a story inspired by her comical canine. Cate lives in St. Petersburg with her husband and their entertaining dog.

The Inevitable

"Honey, in case I don't make it through this, there're some things ya need to know."

"Stop talking like that. Nothing's going to happen to you."

"Ya can't know that."

"David, you're going to get through this okay. I promise."

"Ya can't promise me that, Evelyn. There ain't no guarantees. I'm tellin' ya, I put it off way too long. Now you and the kids are gonna hafta pay the price."

"Stop it! I don't want to hear another word about it. Just try to relax. It'll all be over soon enough, and then you can stop your worrying."

"Ev', baby, that's what I keep tryin' to tell ya. It's about to be all over, and I gotta make sure ya know what to do."

"Not listening. Not listening. Lah-dee-dah-dee-dah-de—Hey, let go!"

"I'll unhand your wrists if you'll keep those fingers outta your ears and hear what I gotta tell ya, Evelyn Mayfield. Promise you'll hear me out. I mean it. *Promise!*"

"Lower your voice, David. You want the doctor to hear you carrying on like this?"

"What do I care what he thinks of me? D'ya think I care what he or anybody else thinks? I ain't gonna be here this time tomorrow, so it don't matter how loud I get!"

"Hush up, David! People are staring at us! You win. I'll listen to whatever nonsense you want to tell me if you'll *please* just lower your voice."

"Okay. Is this better? All right. Here goes: The first thing ya gotta know is there's about three hundred dollars less in the bank than it says in the checkbook."

"*What?* What do you mean, there's three hundred *less*?"

"I thought ya wanted us to keep our voices down."

"David. Lawrence. Mayfield. Where's. That. Money?"

"Now, sweetie, don't get upset. I bought up some life insurance so you'll be okay after… after whatever happens today. I hid the paperwork so ya wouldn't hafta worry 'bout it, but seein' how you're gonna need it soon, I figure I'd best tell ya now."

"Of all the…"

"Lean over a little closer so I can whisper to ya where it is."

"You put it in the *what?*"

"Clever, huh? Only, come to think of it, I should have told ya before now, in case I got hit by a car, or dropped in an elevator, or somethin' else like that. Sweetie, what're ya countin' for?"

"Is that all?"

"No, Ev', now that ya mention it, there's a couple more things I gotta make sure ya know 'bout."

"Get them over with, then."

"Atta girl. That's my Evelyn. Okay. The next thing you gotta know is that if the car breaks down, don't *ever* ask my friend Tony to help you with it."

"Why not? You take it to him all the time."

"Yeah, I know, but not you. You take it to Bob instead."

"That's ridiculous. He's all the way over on the other side of the county!"

"I know, but just swear it to me, okay?"

"I'd rather swear *at* you. This whole conversation is pointless, David. If the car breaks down, how am I supposed to get it to either one of them, and what does it matter anyway? You can take it to them yourself."

"Evelyn, baby, ya promised to hear me out. Just *trust* me. Call Bob, not Tony. In fact, call Bob *before* it breaks down, so he can keep it runnin' good for ya. Promise."

"Fine. Are you through?"

"Almost."

"Thank heaven for that."

"I want ya to tell the kids that I love 'em and I want 'em to take good care of their mama for me. And speakin' of takin' care of Mama, try not to get into any more fights with my mother over th—"

"Don't you dare say it. It's not my fault that she—"

"Mr. Mayfield? Doctor Robinson is ready for you now."

"Evelyn, baby, remember how much I love ya. I'm sorry for everythin' I ever did to hurt ya, and if I had it to do over I never would have... well, ya know. I love ya, darlin.'"

"Come this way, please, Mr. Mayfield. We'll start by taking a full set of x-rays, since your records say you haven't seen a dentist in the last nine years. Just step inside the doorway here..."

TERESA BRUCE

Teresa Bruce writes and gardens in Central Florida, where she contributes to the College Park Community Paper. Her pesticide-free backyard feeds indigenous critters, sometimes yielding enough unscathed produce for her human friends, too. Teaching hurricane preparedness at city, county, and private events, she challenges, "Don't get scared—get prepared!"

Ma Says

"Ma says all things happen for a reason."

"She's right."

"But I don't see no reason for Jacie dyin'. I loved her, Pastor. She gave me my first kiss when I was ten, still a sproutin' boy, and gave me the last one two weeks ago. Her bottom lip was so swollen, it felt like a rock lodged in there. Doctor said her liver was bruised and time was short. But she didn't die so quick for someone hurtin' so bad."

"I'm sorry, Demetrius. I wish I could do something."

"I never hated no one before. Not like I hate the man who fixed Jacie like he did. Killin' her slowly. I tell you what that means."

"What?"

"Means I'm gonna find him and kill him slowly, too."

"Don't say that, Demetrius."

"Ma says pro'ly just a drunk. No reason more 'n that. Don't matter, though. I still aim to kill him."

"I heard what your ma said at the funeral. 'The Lord knows when to take somebody who's cryin' inside.' Jacie suffered despite how hard she tried to hide it. The doctor couldn't do anymore. The Lord had to take her home."

"But nobody could find that man who raped and beat my Jacie, leavin' her in a ditch. No sense in sittin' home with a killer on the loose, I told Ma, so here I am."

"The police are the ones who take care of that."

"Huh. Ma says it just like you. 'Let it be,' she says. But my heart breaks every mornin' I wake up thinkin' Jacie still lives. Then I remember she's gone."

"You aren't a detective, Demetrius. You have to let yourself grieve, but then you have to move on."

"I should grieve, you and ma say. 'I ain't seen you cry yet,' she says. 'Gotta shed those tears or they freeze right o'er your heart. You'll ne'er heal inside like you need to.' Well, maybe I don't wanna heal till I get justice done."

"But you can't find the killer just by watching the people who walk through this park. The detectives know what they're doing, and you have to give up your anger to the Lord. Shed those tears, like your ma says."

"Daddy once said, 'No use spillin' water out yo' eyes when miles o' countryside roads beggin' to be tread on.' Daddy ran the marathon in Birmin'ham every year, but last year he never made it back home."

"I heard about that. I'm sorry."

"Pastor, you gotta stop bein' sorry 'bout stuff in my life. I was eighteen, not no kid. I dealt with that just fine. Me and Ma is fine, and once I kill this man, everythin' be right as rain."

"I hope you don't believe that. Because if you happen to find that man, killing him wouldn't set things right. Not by a long shot."

"Says you. But I know I'm justified. It's justice. Eye for eye. That's in the Bible, so I know you seen that, too. I can track Everyman in this park if he was so dumb as to do what he did drunk, and give him a piece o' metal in the forehead."

"Everyman?"

"Until I know whodunit, his name is Everyman. And every man I see is a suspect. Even you a suspect, Pastor, because you a man. Any man in this town coulda done it, and when I get through with the killer, every scrape, bruise and wound he gave Jacie, I'll give double to him. Then a bullet'll finish him off."

"I've never seen you in a fight, D. You're no killer. I'm telling you, leave this matter to the police. You're too close to it. You might find yourself shooting the wrong person. Either way, you'd go to prison for a long time."

"Them cops pro'ly shoved her file at the bottom of a draw'. If they workin', how come they have no suspect?"

"They can't arrest people on circumstantial evidence. They need proof, even if they suspect someone."

"Ma says I be talkin' like a fool. Says the cops don't get paid for kickin' rocks. They have to sort it out, and not nab no innocent man. I guess I don't want no innocent man nabbed, either."

"I'm glad. Maybe you'll see, in the long run, that allowing the police to do their job will save innocent people."

"I guess I'm goin' 'bout it wrong. Police gotta interview witnesses and stuff like 'at. Hey, I could practice. Pastor Mitchell, where you at the night o' August 23rd, 1984?"

"Well, I was at home."

"Doin' what?"

"I was watching television."

"By yo'self?"

"No, my daughter was there. She likes those Looney Tunes shows."

"Looney Tunes is only on Saturday mornin', Pastor. What you sayin', you makin' up an excuse?"

"No, of course not. We have a VCR tape. That's what we watched."

"Huh. You keep your little girl up so late? Cuz Jacie tol' the police she was attacked at 11pm. What you doin' at 11pm?"

"Well, my daughter went to bed by 9pm. I guess around 10pm I was heading to bed."

"But you ain't married, right?"

"Right."

"So no one was awake who can testify to that, can they?"

"No. I guess not."

"Hm. It's harder than I thought, Pastor. I know you ain't done it, but you ain't got no real excuse either. It must be hard for the police. So far nobody saw anything. Unless Everyman confesses, I don't know how they gonna find 'im."

"That's where trusting the Lord comes in."

"I guess. The more I think on it, Pastor, I don't wanna go to jail, neither. I was gonna marry Jacie someday. She wouldn't want me goin' to prison for murder even to make it right. Ma says it'd make me as bad as the one whodunit."

"I have a lot of respect for your ma."

"She's right most the time, but don't tell her I said that. Jacie taught me a lot of things. How to really love somebody. I'll always love her. Here. You take this."

"That's a wise decision. I'll get it back to your ma."

"Thanks. Say, why you here at the park anyway?"

"Earl David Mitchell?"

"Yes?"

"Will you come with us please?"

"What you want Pastor Mitchell for?"

"He's a person of interest in the Jacie Elton case."

"This is a mistake. We'll talk more later, okay, D?"

"Don't you call me D right now with these men talkin' like you did somethin'. You never said why, Pastor Mitchell. Why you come here to the park where Jacie got raped? Huh? Why! You got no answer?"

"I just knew you'd be here needing someone to talk to."

"You just knew. Ma says a liar comes in all shapes and sizes. Don't worry, Pastor, I still believe Jacie wouldn't want me to kill if it was you. But I think I seen a wolf in sheep's clothin'. I wonder what Ma will say 'bout that."

BRIA BURTON

Bria Burton lives in St. Petersburg with her husband, Brian, and pets, Lance and Ringo. For fun, she runs. Her first publication, "Maribel's Day of Death," was the #4 pick in *FWA Collection #2 - Slices of Life*. She works an office job by day, and is attempting publication of a novel, *Sprinter*.

The Perfect Plan

"This has got to be the stupidest idea you ever thought of. It'll never work."

"Oh, c'mon, Johnnie. You've dreamed up some real doozies. We can do it. Timing is everything."

"Remember last year, Mike? We almost got caught and hauled into the sheriff's office. Ya better not ditch me at the last minute, or I'll kill ya."

"Listen, dummy, I didn't ditch you. I tried to pull you behind a tree, so the sheriff couldn't see us."

"Well, ya didn't pull hard enough. I looked like an idiot starin' into his headlights."

"He believed you, didn't he? Besides, he always expects trouble on Halloween."

"Okay. Okay. I'm in. I don't think only two of us can pull it off, though. Are we gonna let Dave come with us?"

"No way! He's a big blabbermouth, and he'd botch the whole plan."

"What is the plan, exactly? We're takin' a big chance messin' with Old Man Holloway."

"How many times do I have to tell you the details? Is your brain leaking or something?"

"No, but what happens if he answers the door? We're goners then."

"Simple. We'll run if we hear him moving inside. Besides, he's never home on Halloween because he's too cheap to buy treats."

"Okay, but I have a bad feelin' about this."

"Stop worrying! How about we meet at 7:30? Our parents always let us stay out until at least 8:00. That'll give us plenty of time to do it."

"Ya sure ya thought of everything?"

"Yep. Nothing will screw us up this year."

"I gotta go, Mike. See ya tomorrow."

"Bye, Johnnie."

✦

"You made it on time for once. You ready to teach the old geezer a lesson?"

"Yeah. I guess so, Mike. But I still got that sick feelin' in my gut."

"Forget your gut. Who are you supposed to be anyway?"

"Who d'ya think I'm supposed to be? Ya need glasses? I'm Captain Midnight. Who're you?"

"Howdy Doody. See how Mom drew freckles on my face?"

"I sure hope Old Man Holloway doesn't recognize us."

"Will you quit talking that way? You'll jinx us. He won't even see us."

"There's a light on in the living room."

"Yeah, but I already peeked in the window and didn't see anything."

"Are we gonna ring the bell?"

"Nah. I'm pretty sure he's not there. Let's go around back."

"It's really dark back here. Where is it?'

"Are you blind, Johnnie? You're staring right at it."

"Oh. I thought it was painted white."

"On the count of one, we start running; on two, we go faster; and, on three, we shove as hard as we can until it tips over. You ready?"

"I suppose, but I never tipped over an outhouse before. Start countin.'"

"One, two, three! Push!"

"It's not fallin' over, Mike."

"Push harder!"

"Hey! Who's out there? Quit rocking this thing! Wait 'til I get my hands on you!"

"That's Old Man Holloway's voice. Yeah, you really thought of everything, dope."

"Shut up and run like hell!"

Alice Carter

Alice Carter taught English, writing, and journalism in three states. After teaching, she held management positions in corporations and non-profits and then founded a non-profit that provided free school supplies to disadvantaged students. She also created and presented seminars for business professionals. Alice lives and writes in Clearwater, Florida.

A Fitting Memorial

"Please come in, Mrs. Walton. We'll be discussing all of the arrangements for your husband's service today. How old was he when he passed away?"

"He celebrated his 98th birthday a week before he died, and I'm not far behind. I'll turn 97 next month. Hardly worth going home, is it? "

"I don't think we'll see you again for a long time. You seem pretty spry."

"You know, sometimes I think I've lost my mind, but it always finds its way home. Perhaps it's just a sign of senility. Senility does have some advantages, though. Do you know the best part of being senile, Mr. Shaw?"

"I'm afraid I don't, Mrs. Walton."

"I can hide my own Easter eggs."

"Sorry, Mrs. Walton. I had to turn my head to stifle a sneeze. Shall we get on with it then?"

"Since my husband changed his mind about cremation right before he died, we have no pre-arranged funeral plans. I guess we need to choose a casket and select the date and time for his service."

"That's right. Do you want to see the plans we offer?"

"No. Let my sons take care of that. I'll handle everything involved in getting him ready for the viewing."

"We've already prepared his body, so tell me whether you want an open or closed casket."

"Daniel always liked being the center of attention, so leave the casket open."

"Open it is. You have only one more choice to make. What clothes do you want to use?"

"Do the deceased usually wear suits for these services? I've always had an aversion to funerals and have rarely attended one."

"The family often dresses a male in a dark suit, but you don't have to follow that custom."

"Daniel hated suits and only wore one on special occasions, like our wedding day. Most days he wore jeans and a comfortable shirt. Would it be all right to use some of his old clothing? I'd feel better if we could."

"You knew him best, Mrs. Walton. We'll use whatever you choose.

"I brought some things along in the car, just in case. I'll go get them."

"I'd be happy to do that for you, if you give me the keys."

"No, I want to surprise you, Mr. Shaw. I'll be back in a minute. Make that five minutes. I don't have the same zip that I used to."

"I'll wait for you at the door then."

"Well, here it is. My sons and I settled on the outfit in this garment bag."

"Let me carry tote bag you left on the landing."

"Thank you, Mr. Shaw. What do we do now?"

"Only one thing left to do, finish his preparations for viewing. Shall I find your sons?"

"I want to say my final good-bye alone. It will be easier on me, if they're not in the room."

"Let's see the clothes. What in the......? I've handled thousands of funerals and have never seen anything so unusual. Are you certain this is what you want him to wear?"

"This is exactly how I want to remember him."

"It shouldn't take long. Please have a seat by the door while I dress him, Mrs. Walton."

"I might not know much about funerals, but I do know Daniel would prefer me to dress him. If you like my work, maybe you can hire me as an assistant."

"What's wrong, Mrs. Walton?"

"I can't seem to stop crying when I see him all dressed up like this. He looks exactly like he did when he performed. Daniel would be delighted, if he could see himself now. Do you have any tissues handy?"

"Please take the whole box."

"If you'll hand me the tote bag, I'll add the finishing touches."

"Maybe I will hire you, Mrs. Walton. You've created a masterpiece."

"Daniel always relied on me to get him ready. He loved clowning, and I loved making his costumes. His favorite part of the routine was a silly exit that would 'leave 'em laughing.' This should do the trick, don't you think?

"That orange hair, bulbous nose, and pumpkin costume with a flower water squirter should get a laugh from everyone--a fitting memorial for him."

"And a final exit that would make him proud."

ALICE CARTER

Alice Carter taught English, writing, and journalism in three states. After teaching, she held management positions in corporations and non-profits and then founded a non-profit that provided free school supplies to disadvantaged students. She also created and presented seminars for business professionals. Alice lives and writes in Clearwater, Florida.

Blind Tiger

"Young man, yoo whoo, young man…"

"Yes ma'am. Can I help you?"

"Indeed you can. I want two of your best tickets to the Blind Tiger concert."

"One moment, please."

"My, you have a lot of buttons on that…."

"Ma'am, I don't see a Blind Tiger concert scheduled."

"Oh, look again. I know it's there. My kids have been talking about it for weeks. I'm going to surprise them with tickets."

"One moment… I'm sorry. I still don't get any hits for a Blind Tiger concert anywhere in Florida."

"Did you spell it correctly? B-L-I-N-D T-I-G-E-R."

"Ma'am, I know how to spell. The concert you want just doesn't exist."

"It has to. My kids love this band and know everything about them. Try again."

"That's not going to change anything, Ma'am. I'm sorry."

"Don't be difficult, young man. Just punch some more letters into that computer *thingee* and get me my tickets."

"Ma'am, I could key names into this *thingee* all day, but it's not going to produce a concert that doesn't exist."

"Fiddlesticks. It's in there somewhere."

"Oh, wait a minute... "

"See, I *told* you it was there."

"Ma'am could it be the *Def Leppard* concert you want tickets for?"

"Yes, yes, yes…that's it. I knew it was some type of a cat with an impediment."

PATRICIA CHARPENTIER

Patricia Charpentier, author of *Eating an Elephant: Write Your Life One Bite at a Time,* teaches, writes, edits and publishes personal and family history. A sought-after presenter, Patricia speaks throughout Florida and South Louisiana and offers workshops and ongoing courses—including online classes—in Central Florida. Visit her at www.writingyourlife.org.

Acerbic

"Unacceptable! My time is of value, too. Why aren't you complaining?"

"I was told the doctor was running late when I signed in."

"This is ridiculous. I've been waiting more than twenty minutes. My appointment was for nine fifteen. What time was your appointment?"

"Well, I'm not sure; I think nine thirty, why?"

"It's better if everyone is out of sorts. I can complain for you, make something up, like your dog is in the car, sick and needs to be taken to the Vet."

"Reading here is as enjoyable as anywhere."

"Boy, you people are annoying, must you be so perky and pleasant?"

"You're upset. Why don't you thumb through a magazine? There's a travel article about Hawaii in this one. Have you been there?"

"You think looking at pretty pictures of places I can't afford to travel to will help me... what? Be happy I have to wait for a man, I pay to tell me I'm sick. And looking at colorful advertisements won't help either. I'm Acerbic. My parents and grandparents, on both sides, were Acerbic and proud of it."

"Acerbic? Is that … American or … a religion?"

"Acerbic is a way of life. You got a problem with that? Our dispositions are generally crabby. We find fault in others quickly and enjoy being sarcastic."

"Golly gee, everyone feels crabby from time to time."

"*Golly gee? Golly gee*, we've been sitting here over a half hour. Can't you pretend you're a little annoyed? That wing back chair looks awful uncomfortable. These doctors are all the same; think they're better than the rest."

"His nurse said the doctor had an emergency, it sounded serious. Are you really Acerbic?"

"Our whole neighborhood is Acerbic. We don't like friendly. People yell, 'Don't park in front of my house, jerk' and threaten, 'If your dog pees on my grass, I *will* call the police!' Although things are changing. Someone, I can't find out who, moved my garbage pail out of the street on a windy day."

"You don't mind if I read my book?'

"Of course I mind. I get it. Why not say shut-up? Add please if you have to. It's easy; watch my lips, 'Will you please shut-up!' ”

"No, tell me about your life."

"Actually I had a great childhood. We owned a small cabin not far from Route 95 below the Georgia border. Dad named it Acerbia. It was a retreat where we could be sour and discontent on weekends and during vacations. You know, say nasty things about neighbors and relatives."

"Was that fun?"

"Are you kidding, of course, the best. By the way, they call me Unfortunately. I'm Unfortunately Fortunato. What's your name? Not that I care."

"Unfortunately is a first name? And Fortunato your family…?"

"Mom wanted an Acerbic name, nothing cheerful or common like Hope, Joy or Grace."

"That had to be a difficult name for a child. Did she think it was a mistake?"

"No, Difficult and Mistake are my brothers. Mother named them good, too, because Difficult is in prison and Mistake, chronically unemployed."

"Was that a surprise?"

"They still haven't called anyone. All they do is talk on the phone.

Someone else has to complain. You can do it. I like your pink eyebrows."

"My eyebrows are pink?"

"Yea, they match your lipstick, compliment that bluish tint in your hair, and look cool on a woman your age."

"My hair isn't blue! I'm not that old."

"Isn't that book you're reading in large print?"

"It's easier I don't have to remember my glasses."

"Most seniors get a little forgetful. It's normal, not a problem unless you can't remember what glasses are. You know glasses magnify things, right?"

"I know what glasses are for and I didn't forget them. I *do not* need them to read a large print book."

"Did you hear that? The receptionist called Ms. Fortunato. That's me, Unfortunately. Doc's ready for me. Have a rotten day."

"You too, and my eyebrows aren't pink!"

 ## Claudia Carol Chianese

Claudia started to practice writing in 2008 when she and her husband retired and moved to Florida from New Jersey. She has a BS from State University College at Oneonta, New York, a MS in Education from Lehman College, Bronx, New York and has worked in sales, training, and education.

Dental Work

"Hey, Ralph, you're back. Thought you was spending the whole summer on that lake up north at your old war buddy's fishing cabin."

"Planned to, but my teeth got to bothering me, so I come home. Going to see about getting me a new set tomorrow."

"You notice they repainted the benches along here while you was gone?"

"Yeah. Looks nice."

*****

"You done it again, Ralph. Don't know why I'm playing checkers with you today, the way you winning most games. How come you been working your mouth funny all afternoon?"

"Teeth bothering me."

"I thought you got yourself new ones a couple weeks ago."

"I did. They wasn't bad at first, but last few days, I'm not so sure. Best see about getting me new ones tomorrow. You want to play another game?"

"Better not. Agnes's expecting me home. Ever since we went to England them two weeks in June, she has it in her head to have us tea and those little sandwiches sometimes. Today's one of her some-times, so I'll see you next time we're in the park the same day again."

*****

"Squirrels running up and down the trees a lot today, Ralph, don't you think? That mean something weather wise?"

"Not that— Dang it!"

"What's the matter?"

"I near spit my teeth out again."

"Gee, Ralph, you been having trouble with your teeth fitting right the whole year I knowed you. You ever think about finding yourself a new dentist?"

"Dentist? I don't need no dentist. No insurance for that since I retired, anyway. I get my teeth from my brother. He's an undertaker, and we don't see his customers got any more use for them, so he gives them to me."

KAYE COPPERSMITH

Kaye's been "writing" since age five, coming home from kindergarten to regale her mom with impossible stories. Mom thought she'd outgrow it. She didn't, was published at twenty-three. FWA's Editing Service's senior editor, Kaye teaches writing groups the mechanics that tighten and punch up characterization, plot, pace, and emotional response.

The Wedding Journey

"Oh, Ma! I can't remember being so joyous. Did you feel like this when you were going to your own wedding?"

"Nope. I was mostly relieved I'd never have to go home. My Pa drank and would beat us sooner than look at us. I ran away. I knew I'd never have to mess with that again."

"Ma, how'd you come to meet Daddy?"

"I saw him sometimes at the Trading Fair. We lived on Cardin Mountain and he lived across the river near Greasy Creek. Once when we was fording the river's shallow spot I spied him on the other side. That ford had a deep spot with a bad current and walkers had to jump from one log to the other over the hole. I waited to be last to cross and caught Young's eye. Then, on purpose, I slipped and fell into the hole and got yanked downstream."

"I figured Young'd jump in and he did. I told him to pull me on the far side so we'd have a chance to talk until Pa came. While we conversated about who we were and such, I saw him looking at my bosoms through the wet dress. I hadn't planned on that, but it made him get all jittery and I knew he liked me. When Pa came, Young said he'd look for me later. By the time we got to the fair, I was mostly dry and Pa let us go on our own. I spotted Young waving at me, and the next thing I knew we was walking together as if I had known him forever. He held my hand."

"He bought me lemonade and I figured any fellow who had that kind of spending change was a straight catch. Plus, he was mighty handsome. His family seemed nice, too. He wasn't afraid of his Pa."

"Two days later Young come to visit, but Pa ran him off. Then Pa left and when he came back he said it was time I's getting hitched, so he'd promised me to his friend's son. For the first time I stood up to him. I wasn't gonna marry no one I didn't cotton to. He laid me low with his belt saying I had to stay in the back room with no food or nothing until I agreed. He threatened to thrash me every day."

"Oh, Mama!"

"Ma told me to agree and she'd take care of everything. We never saw Pa strike my mama. I think he really cared for her. Ma brought out a jug she'd hid and let Pa drink it all. While he was sleeping it off she told me to pack some things, take the horse and git. She said leave the horse at the ford. Rex would find his way home. Ma stood next to the horse and called me Miss Annette Miles like a grown woman. She said rich gals and poor gals had the same precious treasure. It could only be give once, so choose a man who deserves it. With that she slapped ole Rex's rump and off I went into the night."

"By the time I got to the ford the moon was full up. I got the notion to let the horse cross the river for me. I wouldn't get wet and he'd step over that hole. At the other side I laughed 'cause maybe it wouldn't be so easy for Rex to get back. But Rex was so ugly everyone knew where he belonged. Then I felt bad 'cause maybe Pa'd take out his mad on my brothers. I was fifteen, but I figured my brothers being fourteen and thirteen could leave too, since boys was able to take care of themselves."

"By the next afternoon I found Young's place. His mother, Mama Maddy, asked what I come for. I told her I come to marry Young. Then she asked if I was in trouble. I didn't understand what she meant so I answered yes! She said I'd have to wait 'cause Young'd gone hunting. I asked her if I could do some work for my stay. She sent me to Ferris and Mabel's."

"Mama! You hate Mabel!"

"I didn't hate her then. Didn't know her then. I stayed a week until the fellas come back. I told Mabel I was 'in trouble' and she gossiped how I was a low, immoral girl and Young was stuck with me. Poor Young! By the time he got home he was scorned and laughed about. That's why I'll always hate that ugly Mabel."

"Poor Mama. Your Pa hurts you then your intended family insults you."

"Don't fret about it. I've had a good life."

"Was Daddy mad when he got home from hunting?"

"Naw, he was glad to see me. I explained and he said he'd be proud to marry me. He made sure everyone knew I was still a good girl. Mama Maddy apologized because she misunderstood. She said it didn't make no difference why Young wanted to marry me, 'cause I was welcome under any reason. She invited everyone for supper the next day. In front of the whole family Young proposed like it was all his idea. That nasty Mabel never apologized saying if I was so stupid to say I was in trouble I deserved the bother."

"Mama? Were you scared when you were alone with Daddy?"

"On our wedding night, we had the house to ourselves. When your father took off my nightgown and kissed me, I started to cry. He asked the same question. I told him I wasn't scared of *him*. I'd never felt so safe and loved before, and I was scared it would go away. He told me he would do his best to keep me feeling safe and loved. And I have that feeling each time I lay my head next to his."

"I'm glad you feel safe and loved, Ma."

"I do, so don't agonize over it. You know how I feel about your father. Loving a man makes your life worth living."

"Mama, what makes you happy?"

"When your father puts his arms around me. I feel like the world can't reach me with all its pains and woes. Your father is the first person besides my own ma who I trusted."

"Did you ever see your folks again?"

"When I had Winn and was pregnant with you I saw them at the Trading Fair. Ma wanted to hold Winn, but Pa said we was 'abhorrent to his sight.' Me and mine should never darken their path again. Ma blew a kiss. I saw them sometimes but kept out of their way. It wasn't never gonna be different, so I didn't let myself think about them. Ten years later I heard Pa got liquored up, fell off Rex and died. My youngest brother Shane took Ma to Missouri to live with him. I wonder if she's still around."

"Hey, girl. This is your wedding day! We shouldn't ruin it by hashing up old hurts."

"Mama, I'm happy for getting married. But also for hearing about your happiness."

"Remember the joy, girl. You'll need it."

Patricia Crumpler

Patricia Crumpler is a native Floridian, and a retired art teacher/ librarian. She designs and sews Civil War garments. She produces watercolors and illustrates her own children's stories. She belongs to a great critique group and recently won a children's story contest. She lives in Parkland with her husband and three dogs.

All Wrapped Up

"Don't you think the blue paper with the little penguins would be better for your sister's gift?"

"That might be too cutesy for a twelve-year-old. This is fine."

"I don't know, Don. I'd have adored it when I was twelve. I'm just saying."

"Hand me the scissors. This will go faster if you don't keep challenging everything I do."

"You asked for my help. Am I right?"

"Yeah, yeah, I'm sorry, hon. But the closer we get to Christmas, the more stress I feel."

"Why should you feel stressed? I'm the one meeting your parents for the first time. Or am I?"

"Baby, we discussed this already. I just don't think this is the best time. Here, you do the wrapping. You're much better at it than I am anyway."

"I don't understand why you don't want me to go home with you. Are you ashamed of me?"

"No, it's nothing like that. Look at that package. It's a work of art. You're a natural gift-wrapper."

"What about your mother's sweater? Do you want to use the same paper?"

"Uhmm, what do you think?

"Let's go with the green paper for your mother. Unless you want to use the penguin paper for her."

"Enough with the penguin paper. Just use whatever you want."

"What I want is an answer to why I have to spend Christmas alone while you're with your parents."

"Francine, how many times do we have to go over this? It's not that I don't want you to come with me, it's just that …"

"Yes."

"You know, I think the blue penguin paper would be better for Darlene's gift. Do you mind?"

"But I already wrapped that one."

"It's okay, we have plenty of paper."

"So, you were telling me why I shouldn't come along for Christmas. You've told her about me, haven't you?"

"Well, yes, but …"

"But what? We've been together for nearly a year, and I've never met either of your parents. Now, you're flying home to be with them for three days. Wouldn't this be the perfect time to introduce me? We're talking family here, and …"

"I don't know. Mom's not a very modern woman. She's old-fashioned in a lot of ways and kind of narrow-minded."

"You make her sound like something out of Pride and Prejudice. She can't be that bad."

"She's not … Wait, did you take the price tag off the sweater?"

"Yes, I took the price tag off, Don. I also bought the sweater since you were so busy. You remember that, don't you?"

"Of course, and I told you how much I appreciated it. I never know what to get her, and you have such good taste in clothes. Like that maternity top you're wearing. I would never have thought to put those colors together, but they match your eyes so—"

"You're changing the subject again. How is you mother being old-fashioned a problem?"

"It's just that she's not as accepting of things we take for granted. She's still living in a pre-digital world, if you know what I mean."

"You have told her about me and—"

"Do you want me to hold this together while you tape?"

"Sure."

"And it's a long, uncomfortable flight out to California. Plus a three-hour layover in Cincinnati. I don't know if you should put yourself through that in your condition."

"So, you're only thinking of me?"

"Sure. That and we shouldn't add more stress to our lives at this time. You know how family holidays can be."

"Uh huh."

"That's perfect. The pros at the store couldn't have done any better."

"Yes, I'm perfect in almost every way."

"You are, and I promise that you'll meet them soon."

"Soon?"

"Sure, maybe next Christmas we can all get together. You understand, don't you?"

"I understand perfectly."

VIC DIGENTI

FWA Regional Director Vic DiGenti is the author of four award-winning novels, *Windrusher, Windrusher and the Cave of Tho-hoth,* and *Windrusher and the Trail of Fire*. His 2009 RPLA Book of the Year-winning mystery, *Matanzas Bay*, has been published under the pseudonym Parker Francis.

A Fuelish Choice

"Will the defendant please rise. And remove your face mask."

"But—"

"Mr. Novacks, we're fully protected in this courtroom. Do you see me wearing a face mask?"

"No, your honor."

"The jury has found you guilty and recommended that you receive the maximum sentence."

"But I didn't do anything except—"

"Mr. Booth, please instruct your client that it's not in his best interest to interrupt me."

"Yes, your honor."

"After everything we've been through, you still won't acknowledge the seriousness of your actions. Maybe you need a history lesson."

"Judge Perez, is that necessary? I'm sure my client understands what he did was wrong. He simply made an error in judgment."

"That's almost laughable. Let me ask you a question, Mr. Novacks. What year is this?"

"Are you serious?"

"As serious as your error in judgment. Now, answer my question."

"It's 2016."

"And what state are we in?"

"Judge, I may have screwed up, but that doesn't mean you have to treat me like an idiot."

"Show me you're not a complete idiot and answer my question. What state is this?"

"We're in California. At least what's left of it. And to save time, we're in Susanville, the new state capitol, and it's a Friday morning."

"Good. Now I'll continue with my history lesson."

"Your honor, we've already tried the case, and the prosecution spent considerable time telling everyone of the historical significance of the law. Do we have to rehash it again?"

"When you're a judge, Mr. Booth, and I wouldn't bet your retirement on that possibility, you may address the court in any manner you choose. Until then, you'll let me have my say because I really don't believe your client has accepted responsibility for his actions."

"Yes, your honor."

"As you know, our country was devastated by a combination of factors starting with the earthquake of 2012. Even though the experts had been warning us for years that we were overdue for the Big One, when the earthquake hit off the coast of Los Angeles it seemed to take everyone by surprise. Then the tsunami roared ashore, killing tens of thousands more people, and causing a meltdown of the Diablo Canyon Nuclear Power Plant. The radiation spewed death for hundreds of miles up and down the coast. Hot zones still exist from Sacramento to San Diego."

"Judge Perez, you don't have to tell me about 2012. I lost three family members, and—"

"What did I tell you about interrupting me, Mr. Novacks? I'm already in a very bad mood. We don't know the final death toll from that incident, or from the partial meltdown of the San Onofre Nuclear Generating Station near San Diego. What we do know is all nuclear power plants were taken offline as a result of the dangers they posed."

"Okay, I get it."

"I don't think you do. We might have overcome the loss of nuclear power, but our country's intervention into the Libyan uprising brought all the Arab nations together as nothing has since the 1967 Arab-Israeli War. As a result of that little misadventure, the oil pipelines have dried up, and we're almost totally dependent on coal. Which is the reason you and everyone else has to wear protective face masks."

"But I didn't have anything to do with that. I even joined the Army and served in Bahrain and Saudi Arabia."

"That's most commendable, but let me finish. As you know, gasoline is a precious commodity, and what little we have left is kept under lock and key. Few people can afford $2,600 a quart, anyway. But that doesn't matter since gasoline-powered vehicles have been prohibited since 2015. Even if people found the fuel to power their cars, the emissions would only add to our poisonous atmosphere. And no one will stand for that."

"I hear what you're saying, Judge. Sure, I held onto my car. But the Hummer is just a collector's item. I sit in it, hear the rumble of the engine, and it takes me back to before everything changed."

"Nostalgia is fine, but the reality is that all gas-burning automobiles, lawn mowers, ATVs, boats—you name it—are illegal except with a special license from the government. You don't have such a license, do you, Mr. Novacks?"

"No, but—"

"And even if you did, you wouldn't be able to pay the $200,000 annual fee. Is that right?"

"Right."

"You're fortunate that you live on a farm away from prying eyes and ears. You're aware of what happened to people caught with their collector's items? Mobs have been known to beat and kill these nostalgia types. Even set them afire inside their beloved gas-guzzlers. Terrible times we live in. Did you think of that when you stole from the Strategic Storage Depot where you worked?"

"I'm sorry."

"The state put its trust in you to guard California's precious stores of gasoline."

"What do you want from me? I've already admitted I stole a few gallons. It's not like anyone will miss it. There has to be thousands of gallons in that tank."

"You still don't get it, do you?"

"Really, I do, judge. I'm very sorry for what I did and promise never to steal again. You can take away my Hummer if you want. If I can't turn the engine over every once in a while, what good is it?"

"Please, your honor. Mr. Novacks has apologized for his actions. Sure he did something stupid, but consider his background. He served his country in the Arab Wars. He's not a bad man, and deserves leniency."

"I know you have to plead your client's case, Mr. Booth, but in today's world there is nothing worse than a gasoline thief and a polluter. Because of that I'm forced to throw the book at him."

"Please don't, Judge Perez. I promise I won't ever do anything like that again. I ... I don't think I can ..."

"Stop your blubbering, Mr. Novacks. It's time to suck it up and accept your punishment like a man. It's my judgment that before you leave today you will pay all court costs, as well as reimbursing the state for what you stole."

"Thank you, Judge. Thank you."

"And since you're a lover of the old ways, I want to help you relive those days. Upon returning home, you are ordered to drive your Hummer down Susanville's Central Boulevard. I'm sure our residents will be there to welcome you. You're to repeat this every day at noon until you either run out of fuel, or ... or you're unable to complete this sentence for whatever reason."

"No! You can't do this to me."

"Oh, but I can. Take your client away, Mr. Booth. Oh, and I'd collect your fee before you let him go home. Next case."

VIC DiGENTI

FWA Regional Director Vic DiGenti is the author of four award-winning novels, *Windrusher, Windrusher and the Cave of Tho-hoth,* and *Windrusher and the Trail of Fire.* His 2009 RPLA Book of the Year-winning mystery, *Matanzas Bay,* has been published under the pseudonym Parker Francis.

Sorry!

"Do you realize I was in an important meeting when I got called to your school today, Zoë?"

"I'm sorry, mom!"

"Your father and I both received calls from the guidance counselor requesting we come immediately for an emergency meeting, and all you can say is, 'I'm sorry!'"

"What do you want me to say, mom?"

"I want an explanation!"

"What's to explain?"

"You were wearing cat's ears and a tail when I got to school! For God's sake, what were you thinking?"

"I don't know, but I know I wasn't thinking I hope they call my parents to come to the school!"

"But they did!"

"Mom, I don't know how to tell you this, but I am not popular like you were in school."

"Pardon me for asking, but what in the world does my being popular in school have to do with you wearing that ridiculous outfit?"

"Everything! You had cheering, drama, and Student Council. Not to mention you were prom queen and valedictorian of your class. Most of the kids in the school wouldn't even notice if I were missing from classes for a month!"

"What are you talking about?"

"I'm an Emily Dickinson poem. You know, the one beginning, "I'm nobody, who are you?""

"Now, Zoë, don't be a drama queen! You are not a nobody! You are my daughter—the girl who presently is driving me to distraction."

"Here's the thing, mom. To put it mildly, I possess no social skills. I'm a dweeb!"

"So do you think your sartorial choices today helped to improve your image? Really—footed pajamas, a tail, and cat's ears! How will that getup make you more well-liked?"

"Mom, the popular kids wouldn't be inviting me to their parties even if I wore a Lady Gaga meat dress and showed up in an egg! My friends, on the other hand, had an agreement that we would wear anime costumes today."

"Could you please tell me why before I lose my mind?"

"If you really knew me, you'd know that I love Japanese anime, and I'm in the manga club at the public library."

"And that means you wear cat's ears to school?"

"It means my friends and I decided to wear something to set us apart as a group. We just wanted to belong to something!"

"Did you and your friends ever consider the consequences? My God, if I didn't know better, I'd think Princess Beatrice's milliner had a hand in designing your headdress!"

"I wasn't selfishly trying to draw attention to myself so I could ruin your day at work. I had no idea the consequences of wearing a costume would be that the school counselors would go off the deep end and call you from your precious job!"

"Watch your attitude! Young lady, that precious job keeps food on the table, and in this economy, I cannot afford to be missing meetings!"

"I know, mom, but I had no way of knowing that some kid from Minerville Middle School was going to put a note in her guidance counselor's mailbox telling her that the kids in the anime club at Cassadeega High School were planning to bomb their school! And I certainly had no idea that their counselor would call our counselor to tell her to watch for kids wearing cat's ears!"

"Zoë, don't you see you are very lucky you did not get arrested! Since Columbine, schools are very cautious!"

"I know, mom."

"Your father had to do some fancy talking not to have this put on your permanent record. Don't you want to get accepted into a good college?"

"Yes, I am planning on going to a great college— Full Sail University in Winter Park, Florida."

"That's not an Ivy League School! Have you told your father about your plans?"

"I don't recall him asking me anything about my plans, mom. In fact, until today, I don't remember him saying anything to me in a while. He's usually on the run. Before this afternoon, if I had come up missing, he couldn't have told the cops what I was wearing if he had to!"

"Now that's not fair! Your dad is a busy man."

"I didn't say he isn't. I'm just saying he hasn't asked about my college plans; therefore, we haven't discussed them."

"Well, whoever heard of Full Sail University?"

"Time.com just did an article about the school. Anyone who hasn't heard of Full Sail will soon because 74 of this year's Grammy nominated projects, including all five of the Album of the Year nominees were worked on by Full Sail alums."

"What kind of degree can you get from Full Sail?"

"Mom you are so out of touch with the entertainment world! The school offers degrees in many fields including animation, film, and show production. I'm interested in animation."

"Do you really think your dad is going to pay for you to go to a school for animation after today's debacle? What kind of a career is that?"

"Duh! James Cameron's *Avatar* was a smoking box office success! Money mom, you appreciate profits even if you don't understand me. Walt Disney did quite well with a career in animation if you ask me, but of course, you probably won't ask me. Even though, it's my career we're talking about here."

"No! I don't want to discuss career choices with someone who made a spectacle of herself in school today. Right now, I hear your dad driving up the driveway, and if you're smart, you won't tell him your plans tonight."

"I'll be in my room. Dad wants to see me about as much as Trump really wanted to see President Obama's birth certificate. Besides I wouldn't think of interrupting dad's two-martini veg out! I mean decompression!"

"I'm sorry you see things that way."

"Sorry is the only word for us, mom. In fact, it's the word I have tattooed on my backside."

"What???"

MELODY DIMICK

Melody Dimick, author of "A City of Gulls" and numerous freelance articles for *Strictly Business* magazine, is a former teacher and reviewer living in Deland, Florida. She has just completed a book of poetry with the working title *Backpack Blues* and is revising *RUT?*, her YA novel.

The Catch

"Nothing yet, mom?"

"No Penn. Nothing yet. You should find something to do... maybe clean up the living room?"

"How can you stand it? Every year, it's the same thing. The men go out, and some never come back. And, look at you now...staring out that window. You can't see much beyond the waves caught in our lighthouse beacon, even with the full moon."

"Now, now. Our men will return. Your young man will be with them, you'll see. Besides, you know how important their work is, honey. Without their ships we would starve. It's a risk we have come to know and it's something our village depends on."

"I know. It's just so hard to wait and not to know."

"I'm sure he will be safe. I know it's his first voyage, but your father will be with him and see to his safety...Did you hear that?"

"It's the stairway."

"Jost, is that you? Your brother is out of bed again."

"I know, mom, I'll take care of him."

"Sis, it's them! There're coming!"

"Who's coming, Jost?"

"Father is coming! Father is coming!"

"You say that every night. Now get back into bed, or do you want me to carry you? Oh my God! They are coming!"

"See! I told you so!"

"Mom! Jost was right! They are returning! I can see their lights."

"Now you two have some work to do. We want to welcome father with a clean and tidy house, don't we? Don't worry Penn, you'll have time enough to put on a dress and look beautiful for your young man. Jost, you get back upstairs and cleanup your room. I just hope the catch this season will be enough for our village."

"Mom, a couple of ships have landed. And, oh, look farther on, along the shore, more are descending!"

"Penn, come with me to the door. And, please, tuck in your tail."

"It's so hard to see. Some men are coming this way. They're carrying poles between them. Looks like they've strung the catch on poles."

"Be patient, honey. And, Jost, if you're finished with your room, at least sit still at the table while your sister and I take a closer look."

"I think I see father."

"And your young man. They're together carrying one of the poles."

"You were right, mom. They're back and both are safe. And look at the beasts they've got strung up."

"Big ones. I can hear them squealing from here. Such noise."

"Help us! We are from Earth. We mean you no harm! Please let us go!"

"Penn, what was that sound?"

"Just my stomach, mom."

ARTHUR DOWEYKO

With a PhD in Bioorganic Chemistry Arthur actively researched in the fields of oncology, veterinary medicine, and the design of pharmaceutical drugs. He has published 100+ articles and book chapters. His love of science fiction led to his first novel, Algorithm, a 2010 Royal Palm Literary Contest winner. He has also published several sci-fi/fantasy short stories, and is currently working on the sequel to Algorithm.

The Zoo

"Mommy, I don't like it when they stare."

"Now, now, Micky. They're just curious."

"Yeah, but they scare me."

"Honey, they can't hurt you. The glass is very strong."

"I'm still scared."

"Will it help if daddy comes over?"

"Uh-huh."

"George. Put the cell phone down and get over here."

"Micky, what's going on?"

"George, Micky is scared."

"Well, Kathy, it is his first time here."

"Maybe it would help if you explained what he was seeing."

"Daddy, those animals…they scare me. They keep looking at me."

"Hah. They're as curious about us as we are about them."

"But they look weird."

"Son, they're just different, that's all. For example, see how they eat? They use that long nose of theirs to wrap around the food and bring it up to their mouths."

"Yuk. And their eyes…they're really big."

"Yeah…that's probably because they live in a dark place…not much light."

"George, it looks like a bunch of them just came in."

"Yeah, through that door on the side. Five or six. Oh, wait a minute – it must be feeding time. This little one we were looking at must have been the first to get fed."

"Daddy, what are they doing now?"

"They're bunched up in front of that machine on the wall. That's a food dispenser. See how they line up and take turns? Pretty amazing for dumb animals."

"Mommy, are they really dumb animals?"

"Honey, your father sometimes has a way with words. He meant that he was impressed at how smart these creatures are. Right, dear?"

"Yeah, yeah. Look at the one over on the right. He's waving."

"Wow, daddy. Why don't you wave back?"

"Alright, Micky."

"And mommy, you too…look, look, now all of them are waving at us."

"Stop laughing, George."

"I can't help it. They have to be the ugliest bunch I've seen here."

"They're not so ugly. Long noses, big eyes, even their droopy cheeks…I think they're cute. Besides, the short arms and long tails remind me of some of the wild life back home."

"Hold it a second, I'm getting a call."

"Excuse your father…while he attends to much more important matters."

"Mommy, I'm not scared of them anymore."

"That's the spirit Micky. Just remember, they can't get out of there… where are you going?"

"Just over here. If I put my ear against the glass, I think I can hear them."

"Really? I never tried that. What do you hear?"

"Nothing much, really. Sounds like squeaks."

"Well, honey, they are animals. You're probably hearing them eat."

"Yeah, probably…hey what's that on the side?"

"I don't see anything from here. What are you pointing at?"

"The door. The door to the cage."

"Oh, don't worry about that old door. Like the rest of the glass cage, that door is thick and strong, and it's always locked."

"But, mommy…"

"What is it now?"

"Why is the lock on the their side of the cage?"

ARTHUR DOWEYKO

With a PhD in Bioorganic Chemistry Arthur actively researched in the fields of oncology, veterinary medicine, and the design of pharmaceutical drugs. He has published 100+ articles and book chapters. His love of science fiction led to his first novel, Algorithm, a 2010 Royal Palm Literary Contest winner. He has also published several sci-fi/fantasy short stories, and is currently working on the sequel to Algorithm.

Storm Cloud

"Hi, Jen. It took you forever to call me back."

"Sorry, Eileen. Next time you call, tell them to interrupt me. What's wrong?"

"I talked to Dad's doctor this morning and there's a storm brewing. They've decided to stop the treatments."

"Why?"

"The chemo isn't working."

"Oh, boy. So, what are they going to do now?"

"Jen, they're finished. There's nothing more they can do for him."

"But last weekend he seemed okay, well, at least he wasn't any worse. I don't understand."

"He's been fooling us, Jen. He's dying. It's time to make arrangements with hospice."

"Hey, Grampa. What're ya doing?"

"Hello there, Scotty. I'm painting the background scenery for my model trains. See, this part will go behind the mountain area, and this here's going to be behind the countryside. What do you think?"

"That's cool. Can I help?"

"I suppose so. I think I need some clouds. Can you paint them for me?"

"Sure."

"All righty. Grab one of those brushes out of that jar. Can you reach it?"

"This one?"

"Nope, get a smaller one. Yep, that'll work."

"I need some black paint."

"Black?"

"Yeah, I'm going to make storm clouds."

"But it's supposed to be a sunny day."

"I think it's gonna be raining."

"Raining?"

"Yeah, and storm clouds are black."

"Well, black is too…dark. Storm clouds would be more gray."

"You don't have any gray paint, Grandpa."

"What are they teaching you in school, Scotty? Here, I'll show you some magic. First, a little dab of the black, and then a squeeze of the white. Now, mix them up real good. See?"

"It still needs more black. I want real dark clouds."

"What's with this dark thing? Geez, you're only, what? Nine?"

"Grandpa, I'm gonna be ten next month."

"Okay, you're almost ten. Your life's good. You shouldn't be thinking about any dark clouds."

"Momma says its getting ready to storm. I heard her."

"Now, when did she say that?"

"I just heard her on the phone with Aunt Jenny."

"Oops. Be careful Scotty, you don't want to get paint on your shirt."

"And ya know what? Momma said you wasn't gonna be happy."

"You think your momma was talking 'bout me?"

"I'm pretty sure she was talkin' 'bout you."

"Hmm. Well, don't you worry about a thing. It's a bright and sunny day. No storm's coming. Your momma worries too much. Just like you, painting those dark clouds. You should be painting happy clouds. Now, be a good boy and bring that stool over here, I need to sit down for a minute."

"Scotty? Dad? What on earth are you two doing out here in the garage? I've been looking all over for you."

"Momma, I'm helping Grandpa paint his scenery."

"Scenery? For what?"

"His trains. He's gonna set 'em up out here."

"Dad?"

"Thought it would be good for the boy, Eileen. They aren't doing anyone any good packed up in those boxes."

"But, you shouldn't be out here. It's too hot."

"Nonsense. The heat feels good."

"Dad, you need to rest. Scotty, you run on inside and clean up for dinner."

"But, Momma."

"Scotty, better do what your momma says. We'll work on this some more tomorrow after you get home from school. Run on in."

"All right, Grandpa."

"Dad, what are you thinking? The doctor said you've got to—."

"Got to what, Eileen? Die? Just because the damn stuff didn't work, doesn't mean that I'm going to drop dead tomorrow."

"Dad, I know that. I just think that you need to—."

"While I've got the energy, I'm going to do what I want. And, right now, I want to get this train up and running for Scotty."

"But, Dad.... Okay. If you insist, but promise me you won't overdo it."

"I won't."

"Are you ready for some dinner?"

"Nah, I'm not hungry. You go on ahead without me. I'll be inside later."

◆

"Jenny, I'm so glad you're here."

"How's Dad?"

"He's really weak. He won't eat a thing, and it's all I can do to get those protein drinks in him."

"Where is he?"

"Out in the garage working on that damn train like he's done every morning for the past month. He wanted to finish it in time for Scotty's birthday tomorrow."

"Is he still refusing the pain medicine?"

"He's only taking it at night, now. During the day he wants his mind clear. Every morning, he insists that I wheel him out to that garage. I worry about him out there, but he insists on being alone. I peek in constantly and I've got the alert necklace on him. Don't know what else I can do. The hospice nurse says as long as he's able, to let him do it. They said he'll know when he needs to stop."

"Does Scotty know?"

"That Dad's dying? He knows as much as a nine-year-old can know. The two of them are thick as thieves. Scotty says Dad lets him do all of the hard work, but I know better. We both know Dad's a control freak."

"If it's getting him through the day, then maybe it's not such a bad thing, Eileen."

"Whether the train is done, or not, he doesn't have many more days."

◆

"Scotty, join those last two pieces of track together...then set that engine up here in front of me...we'll test it to see if it makes it all the way around. Start it real slow."

"Wow, look at it, Grandpa! It works!"

"Sure does. Now...let's see what happens in the tunnel."

"Do ya think it's gonna crash in the dark?"

"We'll see."

"Here it comes, Grandpa. It made it."

"Yep, out of the dark tunnel and into the happy clouds. Remember that, Scotty...always look for the happy clouds. Now let's get it moving a little faster."

◆

"Scotty, it's dinnertime."

"Just a sec, Momma. I'm almost finished painting."

"Why, I've never seen red, orange, or green clouds like those. You've used such bright colors."

"I'm making them happy clouds, Mom. Grandpa wanted happy clouds."

MARY S. ERICKSON

Mary S. Erickson is an author from Ponte Vedra Beach, Florida. She enjoys writing short stories and is hard at work on a novel. In 2010 she had a short story selected as a favorite in *FWA Collection #2- Slices of Life*. http://maryserickson.blogspot.com

The Perfect Ending

"Oh, my goodness, this is so funny...Tim."

"What?"

"Listen to this obituary: 'Bernard C. Barnes'... can you hear me?"

"Meredith, I'm sitting at the same kitchen table, eating my eggs and toast. I can hear you."

"Pay attention, then. You've got to listen to the whole thing. You're going to love it. 'Bernard C. Barnes died March 1, 2011. He was born December 9, 1909 in Bristol, Connecticut, the son of Stephen and Annie Barnes, many years deceased. Bernie is survived by his wife, Cicely—.'"

"Not exactly earth shattering."

"Trust me, it gets better. I'll skip some of it. It lists all of his children and stepchildren and grandchildren and great grandchildren—geez, he had a ton of them—then it goes on to say.... Tim, please put down that newspaper and listen."

"Meredith, I need more coffee."

"The pot's where it's always been. Now, here's the good stuff. 'Growing up, Bernie attended—.'"

"I'm really in a hurry this morning. I've got a meeting—."

"Tim, I'm trying to read this to you."

"Please?"

"Oh, for God's sake. I have to do everything for you. It wouldn't kill you to serve yourself once in a while. All right, here's your damn coffee. Now where was I with Bernie? Okay, 'Growing up, Bernie attended no fewer than fifteen grammar and high schools and ultimately graduated from Cornell University where he played baseball, rowed on championship crew and was president of his fraternity. He served in the Navy during WWII. He moved to St. Petersburg from Hartford after retiring from a major corporation as a leading district sales manager, and continued a very active life on the beach.' Tim, pay attention."

"I'm listening. Pass the sugar, please."

"It's right there. Can't you reach it? Yeah, I thought so. Anyway, let me finish this. There's a list of a zillion clubs and activities. Okay, here it is; this is where it gets really good. 'Over the course of his more than 100 years on this planet, Bernie Barnes saw the invention of the light bulb, the telephone, the radio, the automobile, the airplane, the rocket ship, television, the computer, man's landing on the moon, and a gizmo landing on Mars. He lived through twenty different U.S. presidents, both World Wars I and II, Korea, Vietnam, and numerous other conflicts. He wants the record to show that he can't be blamed for any of them.' Isn't that hysterical?"

"Yeah."

"You have no idea what I said, do you? You were reading that stupid sports section while I was talking."

"Of course, I heard you, honey. Bernie Barnes was over 100 years old when he died and he shouldn't be blamed for any World Wars or conflicts."

"Humph. Well, I thought that it was a great obituary."

"As far as they go, I guess."

"Well, it's more entertaining than whatever is on that stupid sports page."

"It's the business section, Meredith. Some people have to work for a living. Hey, get that cat off of the table."

"She wants your crumbs. Come here, Whiskers. And, for your information, you can learn a lot about life by reading the obituary section."

"If you say so."

"It's true. And I'm only at the beginning of the alphabet. And, here's another one. Listen to this."

"I'm sure you're going to read it to me anyway."

"'Douglas Michael Castle died on March 6, 2011 at the age of forty after twenty years of chemical dependency. A great athlete, Doug was a strong tennis player, loved golf, and was an award-winning bowler. He is survived by his parents, brother and his beloved fish, Fancy.' Isn't that great?"

"Is there any more jam? This jar is almost empty. Hey! Why are you smacking me?"

"You never listen to me. Get your own damn jam."

"You know, I think you've become addicted to those death notices. It's not healthy."

"I read them for research, Tim. I'm writing your obituary. I'm still searching for the perfect ending."

"Very funny."

"You never know. Your time may be up sooner than you think."

"I'm not laughing, Meredith."

"Seriously, I've been looking for just the right words. So far, I've come up with the following: Everybody thought his wife was a saint for putting up with his obnoxious behavior."

"Ha, Ha. Now you're funny, Meredith. You know you love me. Whoa, look at the time. I've got to run. Keep that damn cat off the counter while I'm gone."

"That damn cat will walk wherever she damn well pleases."

"You've got to keep her off the counter. It's disgusting, Meredith. Well, I'm out of here. See you later tonight."

"Don't slam the door…. And, you let the door slam. What a pain in the ass. Don't you worry, Whiskers. You can do whatever you want. Here's some milk, little kitty. You drink it up while I finish reading these obituaries.

"What do you know, I've found another one. Listen to this, Whiskers: 'Daphne Montgomery Shuman departed this earth on March 3, 2011. In addition to being a teetotaling mother and an indifferent housekeeper, she was a board certified herbalist specializing in poisonous and medicinal plants. She would like to point out, posthumously, that although it did occur to her on more than one occasion, she never spiked anyone's tea.'

"I love this one. What a gem. 'She never spiked anyone's tea.' Hmm, I've never seen poisoning listed as a cause of death. What do you think, Whiskers? Will that work? Nobody would ever suspect it. Yes, I think I've found my ending.

"How's this sound? Timothy Roscoe Gibson died March 20, 2011 of unknown causes. He is survived by his wife of nineteen years, Meredith, who was a saint for putting up with his obnoxious behavior. Yes, I think that sounds perfect."

MARY S. ERICKSON

Mary S. Erickson is an author from Ponte Vedra Beach, Florida. She enjoys writing short stories and is hard at work on a novel. In 2010 she had a short story selected as a favorite in *FWA Collection #2- Slices of Life*. http://maryserickson.blogspot.com

The Breakfast

"Do you have any seats that aren't near the door?"

"Right this way."

"Oh that's much better, thank you."

"I'll have eggs Benedict, toast and coffee, please."

"And for you ma'am?"

"I'll just have some water."

"I thought you said meet me for breakfast?"

"Never mind. Just water please."

"Are you alright?"

"Yeah, I'm fine."

"Why did you ask me out to breakfast if you weren't going to eat?"

"Never mind. I just don't feel like eating."

"Or talking either, apparently."

"Never mind. I said."

"If you say never mind one more time I'm gonna'--- "

"Michael, keep your voice down."

"Oh, now I'm yelling."

"You're not actually yelling, but I don't want people to hear us."

"What is wrong with you? You are definitely being weird. Did you come here to tell me something?"

"Well, kind of."

"Kind of? Natalie, after two years I think I can tell. Sweetie, please just tell me, what's up?"

"Just give me a second. I want to sit here and think. I need silence."

"Here is your breakfast sir."

"That was fast. Thanks."

"Do you need anything else?"

"Some ketchup would be great, please."

"Sure."

"Since when do you have ketchup on your eggs?"

"Since you started acting like a person I don't recognize. Seriously? Since always. But, in case you hadn't noticed, we haven't had breakfast together for a while."

"Your ketchup, sir."

"Thank you."

"So, are you trying to tell me you don't want to see me anymore? Is that what's going on here?"

"No, Michael, not really."

"Not really? What's that supposed to mean?"

"Keep your voice down please."

"Okay. Okay. Is that it though? You don't want to be together anymore?"

"Oh for God's sake, Michael."

"For God's sake, what?"

"Does everything have to be about you?"

"Of course not. I love you, that's all."

"Listen. I wasn't going to tell you, but I have an appointment at the clinic today."

"The clinic? What do you mean clinic? Oh my God, you're sick. I *thought* something was wrong. Why didn't you tell me? Oh, Natalie, I'm sorry. What is it? What can I do?"

"You can go on eating your disgusting eggs and ketchup. No, I'm not sick. But I have to go to the bathroom."

"Now?"

"Now!"

◆

"Are you okay?"

"Yeah, I'm okay."

"Why are you going to the clinic if you're not sick?"

"Why else, Michael? Why else would I go to a clinic if I'm not sick? Now do you get it? I'm sorry, Michael, but sometimes you can be so thick."

"Oh."

"Yeah, oh."

"And so….. I have no say. No say in the matter at all?"

"No, Michael, no say at all. Not everything is about you."

"But can't we at least talk about it?"

"Jesus, Michael, you just don't get it. Do I have to spell it out? It's not yours."

Ria Falkner

Ria Falkner's talents span many disciplines, including, writing, music and painting. A versatile performing and recording artist, Ria is also an accomplished writer. She is a published poet and her story, "A Love Story" won second place in the Royal Palm Literary Awards in 2010. Ria lives in Jacksonville, Florida.

THE DAY WE RAN AWAY

"Mom? That was our exit! We just passed our exit! Right? I'm trying to learn because when I get my license…"

"Yes, that was our exit, Jessie."

"Where are we going then? The outlets? Because I could definitely stand to get some more stuff for summer. Socks, maybe a Juicy tee shirt? Some of those--"

"No, not the outlets."

"Where?"

"We're going to Florida. To see Gram and Gramps."

"Mom! Oh my God, have you lost it? We can't like drive all the way to Florida from Virginia right now! We don't even have a toothbrush!"

"Sure we can. We should be there by midnight. Are you hungry? Let's get some lunch."

"I don't want any lunch! Let's just turn around right here and go home. I really want to show Sara my new clothes, you know?"

"Mmhm …"

"Okay, Ma. What's really going on here?"

"What's really going on is that we are running away. I've had it with your father. All he does is work and play golf. Sleep, work, eat, play golf. He's never home. He obviously doesn't need the two of us anymore than the ocean needs rain. And so, I'm not putting up with any more of his--"

"But tomorrow he's taking me to the tryouts for the all-star soccer team! This isn't fair, moms. I'm calling Dad. Wait! Where's my...I can't find my cell."

"Really? I've lost mine, too."

"What? How could you? Uh, let's think this through, okay? What about Roxie? I have to walk her and feed her soon."

"Let your dad deal with her for a change! He can take care of the dog and the house and himself, too. You'll see. But you know what? He is really gonna miss us when we're gone."

"Please, Mom? Can't we run away next week, after soccer is over? We can spend like the whole summer in Florida. We can take our time and pack all the stuff we need, like bathing suits and make up and--"

"No, Jessie. I've made up my mind. We're going to Florida. And we're going to have a really nice dinner tonight in Santee, South Carolina. Remember that great steak and seafood place there? We should be in Saint Augustine by midnight. Then, we're starting our new life, with --"

"I already have a life! I don't need a new one. Can you please just let me out here and go start your own new life? Look! There's the North Carolina Welcome Center. You can just leave me there."

"I've packed a few things in a bag in the trunk. We bought a lot this morning, and we can buy whatever else we need when we get--what in the *hell* is that noise, Jessica?"

"Oh my god, it sounds like there's a helicopter right over us! Let me roll down the window and—"

"Damn! The car is... oh my God. We've had a blow out! I've got to get off the road."

"Careful, Mom. Slow down. Okay, we're on the shoulder."

"Neither one of us knows how to change a flat tire."

" Look. See that big Shell sign at the exit up there? You stay here, and don't worry. I'll be right back. Just relax...take your hands off the steering wheel. It looks like you're going to squeeze it to death. Look at me, Mom. Give me some quarters. I'll call Dad. He'll come and get us, okay? That's all we have to do, just call him."

✦

"Hi, sweetie. What's up?"

"Oh, Dad! I tried to call you on your cell. I'm at a pay phone. I can't believe I found one that works!"

"Jessie, a pay phone? Yeah, I saw that on the caller ID so I ignored it. So then you called the office, and…"

"See, Mom and I went shopping and we got a flat tire on 95. She didn't bring her cell and I can't find mine, either."

"What the…? How could--"

"I'm at a gas station and she's waiting in the car on the side of the road."

"Don't you worry. I'll be right there. Now, exactly where are you?"

"Um…like the first exit in North Carolina. It says Pleasant Hill."

"North Carolina! Jessie, what in the hell are you doing in North Carolina?"

"I can explain everything when you get here, but it'll take you at least an hour. Hurry up, Dad, okay?"

"Okay, go back to the car. And if someone stops to help you, just get rid of them, okay? Don't let anyone hang around with you, alright, Jess? It isn't safe. I'll be there as fast as I can. All saints above…no cell phone!

◆

"Look, mom. I got us some snacks. I got Oreos, and for you, cheese crackers with peanut butter…your favorite! And iced teas for both of us. Dad's on his way."

"I'm really not very hungry. But that was nice of you. You're a good kid, you know that?"

"Mom? Um…maybe it wasn't such a good idea to run away today anyway?"

"Maybe. You've got Oreo crumbs all over your shirt."

"Dad really loves us. He'd be so sad if we left."

"And I'd be really sad if I stayed. But, well, I don't think you can understand."

"Oh mom…dad just works hard because he loves us. All surgeons work long hours, and they relax by playing golf. It doesn't mean he's not a good—"

"Come to Florida with me for the summer, Jessie. We'll leave after the soccer tryouts. We'll pack all the stuff we need. Then, in August, we'll make a decision, you and I, okay?"

"A decision?"

"A decision. I'll make my decision and you'll make yours."

"What? You mean…like whether I want to stay in Florida with you or come back up here and live with dad? Oh, no! You don't really mean it. You can't do this!"

"We need to roll down the windows. It's getting hot in here."

"I'm starting tenth grade next year. I'm on the soccer team, the year-book…all my friends are here. I can't leave. I just can't."

"Don't cry. Here's some tissue. I know you love your dad, but I don't…anymore. Just come to Florida for the summer with me? We can even bring Roxie with us."

"Well, let me think about it, okay?"

"You haven't said anything in a while, Jess. Are you alright?"

"Uh huh. You dozed off, you know?"

"Oh? Well, now we have to think about how we're going to explain to your father why we're in North Carolina."

"You mean, how *you* are going to explain it!"

"We could tell him that we--"

"How about the truth, mom?"

Oh, no! We'll need to think up a better story than that!"

"Well, it better include why we don't have cell phones with us. I'd like to hear you explain that one."

"I guess I can't, huh?"

"I guess not."

"Dad would hate it if we lied to him."

"Your father would hate it if I told him the truth."

"Decision time, mom! Here he comes."

CECILIA FIRLING

Cecilia Firling moved to Orlando in 2004, after retiring from her job as an English teacher in Northern Virginia. She writes fiction for young adults. She has attended the Iowa University's Summer Writer's Workshop for the last four years, and is a member of an SCBWI critique group in Orlando.

A Mother's Day Conversation

"**Hey, Mom.** Happy Mother's Day!"

"Jenny! I'm so glad you called. Happy Mother's Day to you, too!"

"So what are you and Dad doing for your special day? **Tristan! Can't you see that I'm on the phone?** Going out to eat?"

"Nothing special, Hon. Just puttering around the house. How about you? Any plans?"

"**Marissa, get off your little brother's bike. You'll flatten the tires.** Plans? Boy, I wish! No, Tim went to work. **Tristan, leave the hose alone.**"

"Where are you? Outside?"

"Yes, I came out to check on the garden. The green pepper plants are coming along nicely and . . **I said put the hose DOWN!** . . the corn has tassels already. Oh, and I wanted to ask you about using horse manure for fertilizer."

"Cow manure is better, Jen."

"I know, but a neighbor is getting horse manure for free and offered me some. **Tristan, get out of that tree. I've told you about that before!** So what's wrong with horse manure?"

"Too many seeds from the hay they eat. They don't break down, not even in compost."

"Oh, well I could make poop tea."

"What the heck is that?"

"Marissa, listen to me. We are not running over there. The neighbor's horse manure arrived and she wants to go over there. **Not now. I'll tell you when.** So you put the manure in cheesecloth. That's the tea bag. And then dunk it in water until the poop dissolves; thus poop tea!"

"Eeww! Sounds sickening. So, then what?"

"You pour it over the garden. **Will everybody please be quiet so I can talk to Grandma?** The tomatoes and corn will love it!"

"Really? Wow. Where on earth did you hear about that?"

"I read it online. By the way, tell Dad my cherry tomato plant is doing great. I wasn't sure . . **Tristan! Put down that hose right now! Marissa! Turn off the water and put the hose away.** Where was I? Oh, yea. I told Dad last week I wasn't sure if the tomato plant was going to . . **Tristan! Get back here! You are not allowed over there.** . . make it, but it's really perked up! Mom, can you believe this? It's Mother's Day and here I am yelling at the kids. You'd think they would give me a break!"

"I'll be sure to let Dad know. Perhaps I should let you go."

"What are you guys fighting about now? Knock it off! Go in the house and wait for me. Oh, the kids always act up when I'm on the phone."

"Honey, I think all kids do. You guys did the same thing when you were little, too."

"Marissa! Grab the dog before he gets out! No way, Mom! I don't remember that."

"The three of you would be outside playing and, as soon as I got on the phone, you'd all cluster around me: Arguing, yelling, fighting, and screaming. Everything happened while I was on the phone."

"I don't remember any of that."

"Neither will your kids when they're older. Perhaps you should join them in the house. They do seem to be craving attention."

"I guess you're right, Mom."

"Thanks for calling. I really enjoyed our conversation. You go enjoy the children for the rest of your day."

"Okay, Mom. **Damn! There goes the dog.** I love you. Gotta go. Bye"

"I love you, too, Honey. Bye-bye."

Sharyn Germ

Relocated to Florida by way of Ohio and Chicago to be closer to our three children and six grandchildren, I found the Southern flora and fauna sparked a new creativity in me. So I've written two children's stories, not yet published, but on the county library's website.

3 AM Discourse

"Michael. Wake up. Get up."

"Dad?"

"Michael, whose place is this? Why are you staying here?"

"Wha … what are you … how are you …?"

"Michael, why is all your stuff here. Explain what's going on."

"Dad? Am I dreaming? I must be dreaming."

"What do you mean, son?"

"Dad. You … you passed away."

"Passed away? Nonsense. I'm right here, aren't I?"

"Are you?"

"Stop fooling around and answer my question. Why aren't you home with your family? Where are Victoria and the kids?"

"Dad. I … I don't know how to answer that. I mean … "

"Stop beating around the bush, dammit, and tell me. What the hell is going on?"

"Dad. This is my new place."

"What do you mean your new place? This place is too small for the four of you."

"Dad. It's not for … I mean, it's only me."

"Only you? Why do you need a place only for you?"

"Shit, dad. How is this possible? How is it you're here grilling me at three in the morning. You're dead. You died two months ago. I was there in the room when you took your last breath. I gave the eulogy at your memorial service. I scattered your ashes at the beach, for Christ's sake. You're dead! We're not having this conversation."

"We most certainly are, and you ARE going to answer my question and tell me why you're in some strange apartment instead of being at home with your family."

"You're a ghost, aren't you? Is that it? You're my father's ghost and you've come to haunt me, right?"

"Let's suppose I am a ghost and I am haunting you. In that case, I am going to haunt you until you give me some answers."

"I can't believe this. Even from beyond the grave, you're still a hard ass."

"And you're still a pain in my ass. Now, are you going to tell me what's going on, or do I need to grab a sheet and go 'boo' until you do?"

"Dad, it's such a long and complicated story. I wouldn't know where to begin and …"

"If what you say is true and I am a ghost, I apparently have nothing but time."

"Alright. I'll tell you. This is my new place. I moved out of the house last month."

"Moved out? Why did you move out?"

"Well, it was more like Victoria kicked me out."

"Dammit, boy, what did you do?"

"See, dad? This is exactly why I don't want to have this conversation. It's like every time I've tried to tell you something difficult, you go on and make it harder. You're impossible to talk to."

"If I'm impossible to talk to, it's because you can never just get to the point. Now, tell me. What happened and why did Victoria kick you out?"

"I don't want to tell you."

"Why not?"

"Because …"

"Don't 'Because' me. Just tell me."

"That's the thing, dad. I don't feel comfortable telling you about my failures as an adult."

"What failures as an adult? You've always been successful at everything you do."

"No, dad. I haven't. You only know about the good stuff that's happened. You don't know anything about the bad stuff going on in my life."

"Bad stuff? What bad stuff? Why wouldn't you tell me everything?"

"I'm not sure I can explain it. I'm not sure you'll understand."

"Try me."

"It's just that ... my whole life you've been nothing but supportive. Yes, you were always brutally tough on me with your love, but at the same time you were always encouraging and positive with me. You taught me to dream big. You made me feel like the most important kid in the world. You made me feel like I can do anything. You were ... I mean, you are my hero."

"So what's the problem? If you feel that way, then you know you can come to me with anything. Why now do you feel you have to keep secrets from me?"

"The problem is that in all my life, from the moment I could first understand what you said, to that final moment in that hospital room where you told me not to be afraid of losing you and that everything will be alright; in all that time, not once did you ever tell me you were disappointed in me. I've racked my brain high and low, and I can't recall an instance or memory where you ever told me you were disappointed in me."

"So what are you getting at?"

"What I'm getting at is that I couldn't face hearing you say that to me now as an adult. I couldn't find the nerve to tell you about how I lost the passion in my relationship with my wife, and how I ended up finding that passion in the arms of another woman. I couldn't stand the notion of explaining how my career had come to a grinding halt because rather than being smart, I decided it was best to be a smart ass and piss off the wrong people at work. I dreaded explaining how rather than learn from you and follow your lead, I've simply been frivolous with my money and am living paycheck to paycheck. The boy you raised to be a good father and faithful husband, the man who was on the corporate fast track, your son with the six-figure salary; that guy is just a myth in your own mind. A myth I helped fabricate because I was too afraid of what you might say or how you would feel. Don't you see, dad? I'm not the person you think I am, and the notion of you being disappointed in me is absolutely devastating for me."

"I see."

"Do you? Do you really?"

"I see that I failed you as a father."

"Wait. What?"

"I failed you, son."

"No. No you didn't. On the contrary, you were the best dad anyone could ask for."

"Well, if you feel that my approval is what you need to define yourself as a person, then I didn't do a good job in explaining that's complete horse shit. I've always been proud of you, but I never expected you to be perfect. No one's perfect. I'm sorry I made you think you need to live up to such an impossible standard."

"It's not that. It's just that …"

"It's just that what, Michael? Regardless of whatever my initial reaction would have been, nothing could change the fact you're my son and that I love you no matter what. I may not have condoned your behavior, but as my son, you would always have my help and support to get through what you were facing."

"I just feel like everything you know about me is a lie."

"I know my love for you is not a lie."

"Wow, Dad. I don't know what to say."

"You don't have to say anything. Like I told you before, don't be afraid. Everything will be alright."

"…Dad? DAD! Come back, DAD!"

Gil Gonzalez

Gil Gonzalez is an author, writer and blogger. Originally from Miami, Gil now resides in Tampa, FL with his wife Lee and his two children. Gil is an alumnus of Tulane University, and is also an avid sports fan, tech geek and music lover.

And You Thought You Had a Rough Day?

"Katie! You look like something the cat dragged in!"

"I feel worse, Frankie. I want a glass of whatever you're drinking."

"Honestly, darling. I wouldn't waste a glass of this Mondavi on you in your current state of disrepair. But I have a better idea. Garçon, oh Garçon."

"Would you cut that out. You know Bruce hates it when you call him that."

"Au contraire, he loves the attention. He just protests to keep it going, darling. Right, Bruce?"

"Whatever. What can I do for you, Katie. Seeing as how our resident snob refuses to behave like us commoners."

"I was going to have a glass of whatever he's having, but I think Frankie has something special in mind."

"Well, do I ever. Bring her a snifter of Courvoisier XO. She needs something to save her day."

"Bad day, Katie?"

"I've felt worse, but I don't remember when. I feel like something the cat threw up."

And You Thought You Had a Rough Day?

"Be right back. Frankie's right, the XO is a treat. Best cognac we carry."

"Are you pregnant, Katie?"

"Hell, no. Can't get pregnant when your hubby isn't around."

"So, what happened? Why the melting makeup, wrinkled garb, and overall bad fashion day?

"Shall we start with cracking my head open before I was dressed?"

"It's a start."

"Toast smelled like it was burning so I peered into the toaster, POP, toast flies out into my face, I rear back, back of my head slams into the underside of the cabinet."

"Ouch. That's gotta hurt."

"You have no idea. So I stumble over to the coffee pot and as I'm pouring, the lid fell off. Hot coffee all over me, the floor, the clean dishes in the strainer."

"Oh my God. Girlfriend, you should have crawled back into bed and pulled the covers up over your head."

"I would have, but I had to see the ADA regarding my rape case. And I had classes after that."

"And how did that go?"

"She said the defense attorney is trying to suppress the knife as evidence."

"How so? He sliced you with it when you fought back."

"I don't know. The lawyer's trying, okay? She said that's why he earns the big bucks."

"Well, the asshole is going down. We know he's the Leesburg rapist. The reported count is what seven women?"

"I hope we convict. But it's discouraging to consider the alternative. If he gets off, none of the other women are going to want to testify. The trials are brutal to the victims. Enough about that. So, how was your day?"

"I am not letting you off the hook with just that little bit, darling. But let me tell you. I had to deal with Ms. Maddie Boviny. I would call her a stupid cow but that would be offensive to cows everywhere."

"Johnny's aunt? She is such a--"

"We know, sweetums. Hopefully somebody will burn the nest before that bitch can reproduce."

"You're terrible."

"Me? She gave me a hard time down in the office because I sent Johnny down for being a weenie wagger. He pulled it out right in class and started chasing the girls!"

"Oh my God. Why did she give you a hard time?"

"Claimed it was my 'gay' influence that provoked him. Hah! That kid has been a pervert for years. Imagine, accusing me of being gay."

"Frankie, you are gay."

"It has nothing to do with Johnny's behavior. Am I not the best second grade teacher you have ever known?"

"The best."

"Besides, she's the biggest Lickalottapuss around."

"She's a what?"

"A lesbian dinosaur, a lickalottapuss."

"You are...Oh my god."

"Made you laugh. Now tell me about the rest of your day."

"This cognac is really good."

"Katie."

"All right. All right. Next, I was heading to back to my classes and my tire blew out. I was up on the other side of Mount Dora and couldn't get a signal. So I started walking."

"Why not just stay there and wave down the first guy who drives by?"

"I tried that. For thirty minutes. No one stopped and the heat index must be breaking into the triple digits. Sweat was rolling down my face, my sides, pooling in my pantyhose. I started walking."

"Get out! No one wears pantyhose anymore. You should have stuck out your thumb. Someone would have given you a lift."

"Not after the assault. I'm just not comfortable. Male strangers make me extremely uncomfortable."

"Sorry. I understand. That's why I gave you the pepper spray."

"So then my heel broke."

"No way. You really should have gone back to bed before you ever started this day."

"Well now maybe you understand the melting makeup and the bedraggled look. Stop rolling your eyes at me."

"Darling, you are...there are no words. What would you do without me to set you straight?"

"Straight doesn't seem like the right word. Without you, Frankie? Life would definitely be boring. You do have a way of making me laugh. And this brandy? Fantastic. It's the perfect solution."

"Told you so. So did you get the tire fixed?"

"No, I had AAA pick up the car and I took a cab to the school. My classes were almost over, Principal Beckwith raked me over the coals, 'Why didn't I call, yada yada yada.' And then David called and said he wouldn't be home until next weekend."

"Ah, another week of lonely nights, lonely days."

"If you start singing the Bee Gee's, I will scream."

"Hey, I sing a pretty good Maurice Gibb."

"I just don't need the reminder of how little I am getting from my new husband."

"Baby, you were practically uncharted territory before he made an honest woman out of you."

"Was not."

"Oh, please. Virgin Forest. At least you found yourself a lumberjack."

"God, I love you Frankie. Take me home so I can throw those covers over my head and not come out for twenty-four hours?"

"You got it, Katie. Let's blow this popsicle joint. Garçon, check please."

"Sorry, Bruce."

DONA GOULD

Dona Lee Gould, Editor, Author, Book Store Owner, leader of FWA's Manatee Writers Group. I write fiction and nonfiction. Currently the editor of *Plotting Success*, the Sarasota Fiction Writer's monthly newsletter. I've won numerous short story contests, some published in anthologies. I also write for local papers on writing and the art community.

Levels of Service

"ASHES ALOFT. May I help you?"

"This the place that takes care of loved ones, er, remains?"

"Yes, sir. We offer a wide variety of flying services, designed to satisfy the needs of the most discriminating consumer."

"Incriminating? I didn't do nuthin'. She just up and died, the Mrs, that is."

"I said DIS-criminating, sir. So sorry for your loss. Now, how can I help you?"

"Well, uh, this may sound strange. But I promised the Mrs. that we'd travel when we retired. But, somehow, we never got 'round to it, know what I mean? So I guess this'll have to do. What do I have to fork over?"

"That depends, sir. We have several levels of service. We call them 'Altitudes'. The plane can fly high or not so high or pretty near to the ground."

"Attitudes? Are you suggesting I'm cheap or somethin'?"

"Oh, no, sir. I said AL-titudes. Like an elevator can go to the top floor or stop at a middle floor or descend to the basement...up, up, and down, down."

"You say this business in on the 'up and up'? I never cared for heights. We always lived on one floor, a ranch, no going up and down stairs for us."

"That's lovely, sir. As I was saying, we have all levels, ah, Altitudes of service. I'm sure you want the very best final trip for your wife, er, the remains. Oh,

I didn't even mention that we offer special hymn accompaniments for each Altitude."

"Hymns? I don't have to sing, do I? The Mrs. used to hold her ears when I'd croon 'Baby, be good'."

"Oh, no, no. We use a digital sound track. Now for our best ASHES ALOFT Altitude, that's 5,000 feet, we play 'Nearer, my God, to Thee'. We employ a top-of-the-line twin engine Beechcraft King Air. This is a real winner and costs only $3000."

"OMG, whadda you think I am, a sucker? The Mrs. scolded me, said I wouldn't shell out, but I'm no sucker!"

"Now, now, sir. Don't get upset. I know this is a very stressful time for you. Maybe you'd prefer our medium Altitude. We hover at 3000 feet. 'On Eagle's Wings' wafts through the single engine, late-model Piper Cherokee as our pilot executes slow S-turns. Many choose this very affordable level at only $1500."

"Fifteen hundred dollars! I dunno. This is much more than I thought it'd be. Sounds like a rip-off to me."

"Well, then, sir, you might like our low Altitude service. We wobble just above the tree tops while the sound system renders 'Rescue the Perishing, Care for the Dying' - that's an old Methodist hymn. Our experienced pilot commands a converted Air Tractor AT-402B crop duster. It was once used for aerial application of agricultural treatments. Now we find it reliable for discharging all types of pests. It's only $100 and you can ride along, too!"

DONNA GUILLAUME

A retired minister and organist-choir director with a private pilot's license in her wallet, Donna's dialogue incorporates her experiences. "Ashes Aloft" germinated from a Note at the end of Erik Larson's *Isaac's Storm: A Man, a Time, and the Deadliest Hurricane in History.* Larson relates how a hurricane scientist spent his retirement at the University of Miami library where he died. The staff contacted the Hurricane Hunters of the Air Force Reserve who dispersed his ashes into the eye of a storm. Contact Donna at guillaumedonna@gmail.com.

A Cat's Perspective

"Catrina! Get in here! I'm writing about pets today and thought you might have something to say on the topic."

"Really? NOW you want my opinion? Didn't have anything to say to me when you were writing that crappy story about the little mouse, even though I'm the world's authority on mice. But were you going to ask me? Noooo, of course not, you are too high and mighty to ask the lowly cat a question."

"Awww Catrina, don't sulk. It's beneath you and I really do need your help."

"Well... I was about to take a nap, but if it's that important to you I guess I could give you a minute. What is all this stuff on your desk? Never mind, I'll lay on this stack of papers right here. Hold on. Ahh, now, that's much better."

"Kat don... you're knocking everything dow... oh, never mind. Anyway, thank you for helping. Catrina?"

"Wrmph, blergh pflump"

"Catrina, do you think you could stop licking yourself long enough to talk to me?"

"God, woman, you are a pest! Maybe if you humans had long, beautiful hair like cats instead of that Brillo pad nonsense on your own head, you would understand that grooming is a full-time job! And it's not like it's any fun for me, you know. You try coughing up a fur ball and see how you like it."

"Catrina, there is nothing wrong with my hair, thank you very much! Besides, I don't give a fig if you groom yourself until the sun rises twice in a day, but it would be nice if you could take a few minutes off to help me out! After all, who's the one that trekked through hurricane winds just to make sure you didn't run out of that kibble you're so fond of? Besides don't think you're fooling me with your whole 'my coat's a terrible nuisance' because it's obvious that you're more vain than a homecoming queen in a tin tiara."

"The hurricane story again. Woman, really? Give it a rest! You'd think you actually got blown away in the storm the way you carry on."

"I ran my car into the mailbox, if you recall."

"As if that's MY fault! I keep telling you to take it easy, stop rushing around so much, and while I'm on the subject, what's with all that jumping around in front of the TV this morning? You looked like you had a flea up your butt and were trying to get it out by shaking it stupid!"

"Jum... are you talking about my exercise video?"

"Exercise, shmerxercise... you should take a page out of my book. When's the last time you saw me jump around lunatic? It's just not dignified."

"Pardon me, Queen-of-all-living-creatures! You know, a little exercise wouldn't hurt you either, or haven't you noticed that your rump is a little over-padded?"

"I'm just big boned, besides I have this long black hair that makes me look fat and I'm exceptionally fluffy. But I wouldn't talk about rumps if I were you. Hey, I'm getting bored. Why am I here?"

"Again, I'm writing a piece about pets and thought you might have some insight."

"About pets?"

"Yes, Catrina, about pets!"

"Me?"

"Who else is in the room? Do you see anyone else I could be talking to?"

"Don't get snippy, I'm just thinking about the question, that's all."

"What's so complicated about the question? I just want to know your point of view about pets! I THOUGHT IT MIGHT BE INTERESTING!!"

"God, get your panties untwisted would ya? I blame all that exercise, crazy stuff, makes you cranky."

"Catrina, I am running out patience, do you have something to offer or not?"

"Hmmm, what do I have to say about pets? Well, I never really thought about it, but humans make good pets, I think. Much better than dogs. They're easier to train and don't make nearly as much mess. Is that helpful?"

"I give up!"

Amy Gump

Amy Gump is currently at work on the novel, *A Witch's Forgiveness* and a series of fairy tales, *Across the Crooked Bridge*. Both are works-in-progress. She publishes regularly on the *WriteStuff* at AmyGump. org. Amy (& her cat) are native to Florida where they battle for creative space with one husband, two daughters and four grandchildren.

Creative Science

"How's your experiment going?"

"Good. It's for the science fair coming up. You want to see what I have so far?"

"Sure."

"Okay. I'm testing to see whether carbon-based life forms thrive better in the dark. Take a look at this galaxy. See that planet? I call it Garpult."

"It's a beautiful planet. You're very creative."

"Thanks. It took me a whole week to create it. Look closely. There are mountains and deserts and seas. I even made flatlands and canyons."

"It's superb."

"Thank you. I did my best."

"It shows. I see you also worked hard on the plants and animals."

"You have no idea. I made everything I could think of, all the way from this simple little worm to this great elephant. Don't tell Uncle Sholk, but his nose was the inspiration for the elephant's trunk."

"I won't tell."

"And then I made the people. Garpultians, I call them. I gave them a plethora of emotions."

"Really? A plethora. You've been studying your vocabulary words, I see. Tell me about this plethora of emotions, son."

"Well, some of them feel good, and some of them feel bad. But they're all important, so even the ones that feel bad aren't really bad. It's a built-in guidance system. They let the Garpultians know what direction they're headed. A primitive sort of GPS."

"Clever. What else did you give these Garpultians?"

"Free will. And, look. I duplicated it all over here on this planet, but I call this one Earth."

"I see they both have their own solar system. I thought you'd keep one in the dark for this experiment."

"I'm not doing literal dark and light. But, yes, figuratively speaking, I'm keeping one in the dark."

"I don't think I follow."

"Okay, so the two worlds are identical in every way. Except on Garpult, I told the people what the plan is. They know me. I let them see me every day. I answer all their questions, and I explained to them that one day, when my experiment is over, they'll be brought here to Shripsiz to live with me forever and be well taken care of."

"And the Earthians?"

"Earthlings. I don't know why, it just sounded better. They're the ones I'm keeping in the dark, so to speak. I've been a little more hands-off here. I introduced myself to the prototypes and told them to pass it on to their offspring who I am and what my plan is, but I must admit it's been like a game of telephone so far. Remember that game, Father?"

"Where you sit in a circle and whisper something to the kid next to you and laugh about how mixed up the message gets as it goes around the circle?"

"Exactly. The message I gave the prototypes has already gotten all messed up. And the strangest things began to happen when the offspring discovered they heard a different message."

"What happened?"

"They started fighting each other. Each were so sure they had the message right. It bothers them when someone thinks something different. They've even killed each other over it."

"Why didn't you stop them?"

"I gave them free will, remember? What's the point of free will if I step in and make them do it my way?"

"Good point. But doesn't it bother you to see them hurt?"

"Of course it does. I made them. I love them."

"And you still think they should have free will? Even though they choose turmoil and violence and—"

"Oh, for sure. You're right, with free will came fighting and disease and sadness, but the Earthlings appreciate beauty and peace and they love to a much greater extent than the Garpultians. The contrast makes them richer. Do you remember the universe I made a while back?"

"Yes."

"No free will there. They had to do whatever I said."

"You said they died of boredom, as I recall."

"They did. They didn't last more than a few generations."

"And the Garpultlings and the Earthians?"

"Other way around."

"Oh, sorry. Garpultians and Earthlings. Are they flourishing?"

"Sure are. They've lasted many generations already. I believe free will is directly related to a strong will to live. In fact, the Earthlings have proven this over and over in their fight to remain free among themselves. 'Give me liberty or give me death,' I heard one of them say."

"And what's your conclusion? I'm guessing the Garpultians are thriving better. They aren't fighting. They must feel quite safe knowing you, their creator. I suppose they have peace of mind knowing all there is to know."

"Surprisingly, no. The Earthlings are happier. Life's mysteries make them curious and give them passion. They're deeper thinkers and much deeper feelers."

"Don't those deep feelings bring sadness? I mean, do the Garpultians even know sadness?"

"No, they don't, because there's no disease, no disaster, no fear, and no conflict. But they have no passion for life, either. They seem to just be going through the motions. I think they're losing their will to live. Not much point in getting out of bed in the morning if you have no questions. No questions, no quest."

"Indeed, son. You can't have a quest without a question. Do the Earthlings ask questions, even though you don't show your face and answer them?"

"Oh, yes. That's the beauty of it. They ask all the time. And they exert a lot of energy searching for the answers. Often, they find the answers on their own, by intuition and by observing the world I created. Sure, they fight about who's right, but at least they care."

"So what have you learned, son?"

"That He's chosen the perfect system for us here on Shripsiz. That perhaps, like the Earthlings, we weren't meant to know everything there is to know all at once. I've learned to trust Him even though we don't see Him face to face like they did in the olden days. I can see Him all over our planet, in the purple sun and the great waterfalls of Corpaldite. I hear Him in the early morning songs of the flying whirplers, and I feel His presence in the love in my chest. I guess that's enough for now."

"Very good, son. I think you'll get an A on your project."

"Can I go out to play now, Dad? I"m toying with a new idea I might use to give the Earthlings another mystery to unravel. You want to see it? It's in the fish pond out back. It's a little something I call evolution'

Kim Hackett

Kim Hackett lives in the Tampa area with her husband, Jeff, and her two children, Kate and Tom. Her short stories have been published in *FWA Collection #2 - Slices of Life* and *The Florida Writer.*

Mom's Visit

"Hi, Mom. You came."

"Of course I came, sweetie. What'd the doctor say?"

"Beats me. I've been asleep like the whole time."

"Are you in pain?"

"Not really."

"Good. How's your dad?"

"Hard to tell. You know Dad, he's like an island. I guess he's doing okay."

"Mindy, tell me the truth. Were you texting while you were driving?"

"Oh, boy, here we go."

"Don't you roll those eyes at me, young lady. Were you or were you not texting when you crashed?"

"Yes."

"Mindy, this is the second accident you've had in six months. You've only had your license, what, eight months? You've got to be more careful."

"Please don't tell Dad I was texting, he'll freak."

"I won't, sweetie. I wouldn't even if I had the opportunity. I can't talk to him anymore. The man doesn't hear a word I say."

"Don't be too hard on him, Mom. He's been through a lot."

"I know. Maybe you could talk to him for me."

"Not a good idea, Mom. I hate it when you put me in the middle. Besides, last time I tried to give him a message he went ballistic on me. It's not fair. You either have to figure out a way to make him listen, or find someone neutral to be a go between. It's not right to ask a sixteen-year-old to do that."

"You're right. You're right. But does it seem like he's happy now? Has he had any lady friends since I left?"

"Oh, jeez. Don't say lady friends, Mom. You sound a hundred years old."

"Okay. Let's see. Has he hooked up with any hot chicks?"

"Just say girlfriends, Mom. Jeez. And no, he hasn't had any girlfriends."

"Any dates?"

"Nope."

"Did you tell him what I said about moving on? He should move on, you know."

"I told him. But he like got all mad at me and told me to butt out."

"How'd you say it? Did you use my exact words?"

"I don't know. I didn't write it down, Mom. Jeez."

"Well, how'd you say it?"

"I said, 'I talked to Mom today and she told me to tell you that it's all right with her if you find someone new.'"

"And?"

"And what? He got all mad and told me to do my homework."

"Maybe you said it in a condescending way. What was your tone like?"

"Oh my God, Mom, I can't do this. Don't worry about Dad. He'll be all right. It just takes time. Can we like talk about something else?"

"Okay, honey. What should we talk about?"

"Let's talk about you. How do you like it there?"

"It's fine. Great, actually."

"Well, it seems to suit you. You look really good, Mom. You like haven't aged a bit."

"Very funny. Your dad looks ten years older. And he's lost weight. Is he eating well?"

"Seriously, Mom? I hardly ever get to see you. Do we really have to do this?"

"Do what?"

"Keep talking about Dad."

"Well, his clothes are hanging on him. And you—you've shot up three inches without gaining an ounce. How often does he fix a balanced meal for the two of you?"

"O.M.G. What'd you expect? After you left, he had to pick up more hours at work to make ends meet. Plus he comes to all my school activities and goes to church like three times a week. He doesn't have time to cook, even if he knew how."

"I should've made you spend more time in the kitchen, helping me. At least you have my recipes."

"Whatever."

"Don't whatever me. It's disrespectful. Oh, good, here comes the doctor."

"Mom, when I leave the hospital, do you think I'll go with you this time?"

"I don't know, Mindy. I tried to find out before I came, but no one would give me a straight answer. You'd think I'd have some kind of inside information now, but I don't."

"I want to go with you."

"Now, Mindy, we've been over this. You know that's not where you belong. Please don't cry. It'll get better for you, dear. Aren't things better now than they were a year ago?"

"I suppose. Mr. Barker says—

"Who's Mr. Barker?"

"My shrink. I told you about him."

"No, you didn't."

"I did, but whatever. He says it's hard enough being a teenager, but that I have added pressures, living alone with Dad and missing you so much."

"Ouch! That one hurt."

"I want it to be like the old days, Mom."

"Me too, Mindy. I'm sorry. Just remember our separation won't last forever. We'll be together again."

"I know. And it's not your fault. I don't like hold you responsible or anything."

"Thank you, honey. That means a lot."

"What are the doctors doing, Mom?"

"Looks like C.P.R."

"They're pounding on my chest. I don't even feel it."

"That's because you're with me now."

"So, do you think I'm going to stay with you?"

"I'm not sure."

"Mom?"

"I'm right here."

"I don't want to go with you, but I don't want to leave you either. I'm so confused."

"Don't be in a hurry, dear."

"Mom, I'm getting pulled back into my body! Do something."

"I can't, Mindy. It must not be your time."

"Don't leave me, Mom."

"I"ll always be right here. You can talk to me whenever you want. You have the gift. Hey, maybe you can teach it to Dad so he can talk to me, too."

"Mom, you're starting to fade. I'm scared."

"Don't be scared. I won't ever leave you sweetheart. I'll be here, waiting."

"Bye, Mom. I love you."

"I love you too, Mindy. And no more texting behind the wheel."

KIM HACKETT

Kim Hackett lives in the Tampa area with her husband, Jeff, and her two children, Kate and Tom. Her short stories have been published in *FWA Collection #2 - Slices of Life* and *The Florida Writer*.

A Government Girl

"Who left the world atlas on the table?"

"Hello, John. Sit down. Sit, please. How was work? Here's the paper."

"Why is the atlas on the kitchen table and opened to Italy?"

"Oh you know our Helen. When she reads, she looks things up. She must have been looking up that place in Italy, the place where that terrible battle's been going on."

"Anzio. Anzio Beachhead."

"That's right. So many of our boys dying on a tiny bit of sand. So terrible. How would you like a slice of hot apple pie while I finish getting dinner on?"

"No pie now, Pearl. And we only have dessert on Sundays, remember? Oh, and I was on my way to the plant this morning, just turning off Front Street when I looked in my rearview and saw Helen going down our sidewalk and through the hedge. She looked like she was heading for town. Where was she going?"

"Let me turn the lamp on so you can see to read. That news print is so small."

"Answer me, Pearl. Where was Helen going?"

"Ah…She was going to the bank."

"The bank? At 7:30 on Saturday morning? It's not opened."

"It was opened this morning, Pops."

"Oh, Helen, good. You're back. Sit down. Talk to your father. Tell him your wonderful news while I mash the potatoes."

"I took a test at the bank this morning, Pops, a government test."

"Helen, we went through this when you graduated from college and wanted to join those women soldiers."

"Waves. They're called Waves, which stands for Women's Army...

"I don't care what it stands for, Helen. You were 19 and needed my signature to join. And I wouldn't sign because there's only one kind of woman who goes into that kind of thing."

"Yes, there is, Pops, a patriotic one!"

"Don't sass me, young lady. Ever since you got that college degree, you've thought you were smarter than me."

"I'm 20 now, Pops. And I don't need your signature to go to Washington this summer and work for the War Department."

"Now Helen, just sit down with your father. Here. Both of you drink some nice iced tea with mint."

"Helen, I know you've taught high school for a year, but you've never been further south than Bristol and no further north that Roanoke. Washington, D. C.'s a big city and no place for a young lady. I can't let you go. For your own good, I can't let you."

"The Government needs me, Pops. An Army recruiter came to Saltville High yesterday and told all us women teachers that the government needs us to do office work, which would free up more men to go over there. See the government has an awful lot of record-keeping and administrative work to be done."

"Don't argue with me, Helen. Your mother needs you here this summer. Look at that huge garden we put in. You mother will need help with the canning. Think how many people we feed all year from that garden. Uncle Otis, Great Aunt Ida. You're helping the war effort right here."

"Now you listen, John. Our Helen was valedictorian of her high school and college classes. Remember this? HELEN SMITH TOPS DEAN'S LIST AGAIN! The government needs our Helen. You said it yourself. Helen's the smartest person ever to come out of this family."

"You're pretty smart yourself, Pearl, but I see your plan of attack now. Helen left the atlas open to remind me of the battles in Italy and you bring out one of her old college newspapers. I feel like my wife and daughter are railroading me."

"Pops, think about Doug Blevins and the Grady twins, all dead before they turned 20. And I'm afraid we'll lose more local boys before this war is over. I have to do my part. I just have to."

"You're not going anywhere until I talk to this Army recruiter and make sure you'll have a respectable place to live in that city. Now who could that be ringing our doorbell just at dinner time?"

"It's the recruiter, Captain Ralston, Pops. He's coming to dinner. I'll get the door."

ELLEN HERBERT

My fiction has won a PEN Fiction Prize, a Virginia Fiction Fellowship, and a Pushcart Prize nomination. My writing has appeared in The Washington Post "Style," First for Women, and literary magazines such as The Sonora Review. One of my stories was read on NPR. I teach writing at Marymount University.

In the Waiting Room

"God, what a terrible morning. Now I can look forward to sitting here all day in this ugly waiting room. I would run out and do some shopping, but I don't dare do that today. Joe might have one of his bad days. Then they'd have to call me, and I'd have to come running back, and I'm just too tired."

"You OK?"

"Not really. I'll probably calm down in a minute. My husband Joe just gave me fits this morning. Now we're late for therapy, and everybody is going to demand full payment anyway. Geez."

"Bad…?"

"Well, honey, I don't know which one of these patients is in your family, but my husband has aphasia along with no use of his right arm or leg. He can't talk, plain and simple. Oh, he can get his message across with pointing and a little writing and a word here or there. But mostly I have to play twenty questions. And I just can't do it some days. And he's so damned hard-headed about some things, and he doesn't always know what I just said. This morning was a real doozy."

"Sorry."

"I'll get over it. But god, this morning he was bound and determined that he wanted something or wanted something a certain way, and he kept doing the same thing over and over, and I asked every question in the world that I could think of, and he just got madder and madder until finally he threw a pen across the room. Oh, not at me, but just across the room. And I stood there thinking, this is my husband who has never thrown anything in anger that I know of for over 40 years. I just stood there, and then I began to cry. I mean, I'm at my wits' end and it's only eight o'clock in the morning. We have to drive about 40 minutes to get here for the nine o'clock session, and there was no way we could finish everything with getting him dressed and me ready and him in the car and make it on time. And I just stood there crying. Then he just wheeled himself out of the room, he just turned away."

"He...frustrated."

"Well I can't even imagine how frustrating. At night I lay awake trying to think what it must be like without being able to say things, or write things, or read. But that doesn't help at times when I just want to throw a plate or anything some times, just like he threw the pen. I mean, I think sometimes that maybe it's harder on me in the end. I've had to take over everything – the bills, the money – and there's more bills and less money. All the housework, getting him here to therapy. And he can't do everything himself, he needs help in the bathroom, the shower, getting dressed, meals, everything right now. On a day like today I think this is hell. ...Have you ever had a day like this?"

"Well, yes but no."

"What do you mean?"

"Well, um, me stroke. I mean, I...stroke. And aphasia, me, too."

"...You had a stroke?"

"Yes, me."

"But you are just a beautiful young woman. I thought you were some other patient's daughter. How old are you, like 20 or something?"

"No, twenty...no twenty...no, two and three."

"You're twenty three. And you had a stroke."

"Yes, me. And your...man...hard, hard, frustrating."

"You can say more words than my Joe."

"Well, word word maybe. But me, two-three. Frustrating! Frustrating! Mad, me too and Joe too."

"I'm sorry. I feel terrible now. I thought you were somebody's daughter. I thought you were here with your mom or dad who had a stroke. I've seen you here in the waiting room, and in the hall, and you don't look like you had a stroke."

"Leg, not bad, arm, not good, but talking, no talking. Mad, me too. Mad! Me, two-three, and what for me? School, no. Work, no. And your...he mad. No talking!"

"I'm so sorry. I really thought you were somebody's daughter. I would have never guessed that you were one of the patients."

"Throw...pen? Me, no. But me, go...room, and throw. Books, all gone. Throw. Me, two-four, two-five, what, what?"

"I'm so sorry. God."

"You, old, sorry, but old. Years and years, talking, and everything. Me, what? Don't know."

"I'm sorry. I didn't really know that people as young as you had strokes."

"Yes! And me, no bad. No...this one, this one."

"Drugs?"

"No drugs, and no...this one."

"Smoking?"

"No...smoking. Nothing me. Good. But stroke."

"I just didn't know. I'm sorry."

"But, OK. You..too, OK. Because me, talking bad bad before, now better. And...Joe, better better too."

"Yes, he has gotten better. I keep trying to think that. But on a day like this I just think I don't have the strength to carry on."

"Yes, yes. Go and go. Me, one-two-three-four-five-six-seven-eight-nine ...weeks stroke.

"It's been nine weeks since your stroke?"

"No no, weeks, no. Not weeks...um...months, months."

"It's been nine months since your stroke?"

"Yes. And better, better."

"Nine months. It's only been one month with Joe. I don't know if I can make it that long. I'm so tired now."

"Yes, go, go. It's OK. Then better, better. Promise."

"Honey, I want to apologize to you. I made an ass of myself just dumping on you like that and I just thought you were a family member like me. I'm so sorry."

"OK, OK, don't worry. I know, I know."

JACKIE HINCKLEY

Jackie Hinckley is Associate Professor Emeritus, Communication Sciences and Disorders, at the University of South Florida. She has published books, book chapters, and numerous scientific articles on the topic of aphasia and stroke rehabilitation. Other writing has appeared in the *St. Petersburg Times*, *Latitudes & Attitudes*, and *Stroke Connection Magazine*.

Lots Of Years A-Leaping

"You have an appointment tomorrow with the eye doctor, Harold."

"Told you, Grace. Don't need glasses. I see fine."

"You're squinting now. Like always. Time to get your eyes checked."

"Go to enough doctors, woman. Don't need no more."

"Face it. Age is sneaking up on you."

"Sneaking? No. It's leaped on my back and wrapped me in a bear hug. Just keeps squeezing, tighter and tighter. Won't let go."

"You saw the urologist today. What did he say?"

"That quack didn't say nothing that made any sense."

"Like what?"

"Said it's a natural part of aging. I have to accept it."

"He's probably right."

"Easy for him to say. He's a kid. Hasn't aged yet."

"Yeah. He barely shaves."

"Right out of college. All he knows is book learning."

"You should throw him over your knee. Give him a whipping. Show him what hurt feels like. See if he accepts it."

"Wanted to, but my knee ached too badly. How 'bout your doctor? She tell you anything?"

"Same old story. Wants to run more tests."

"Doctors do more tests than teachers. We see a doctor tomorrow?"

"See chiropractor Thursday. You gonna let him fix your back again?"

"No. Last time, he tried to twist me into a pretzel. I still can't stand up straight. Have to look at my shoes all day."

"Well, Methuselah, it's time for bed. Think you can haul your carcass out of that recliner? Get yourself to the bathroom?"

"I'm not sleeping in the bathroom."

"You hang out in there so long, I think you're asleep."

"Ha. Don't think Jay Leno will include that in his monologue, laughing girl."

"If you dodder that far, you can make it to the bedroom. You remember the way?"

"Got any more punch lines?"

"Depends."

"Didn't ask your brand."

"You're a real senior citizen comedian, aren't you? Where's my cane?"

"Hanging on my walker. I'll bring it to you, soon as this fool recliner turns me loose."

"Don't know why you sit there. Can't never get up easy."

"Got pills now, Grace. Pills for everything 'cept growin' old."

"Leave them be. Just my luck, you'll take one of them four-hour tablets."

"Them ads say don't use 'em if I take heart pills."

"That's so you won't kick the bucket, Casanova; make me tell EMTs what happened."

"If I go like that, you won't be a lonely widow, Ms. Prude. Men will line up outside your door like at Space Mountain."

"You always said that's how you want to go."

"Yeah. I want the undertaker to work overtime, taking the grin off my face."

"Dream on, senior lover. I'm going to bed."

"Want me to help you undress?"

"You pervert. That's all you think about."

"Not all. Think more about what comes after."

"Forget it. Ain't nothing coming after. Not tonight."

"Figures. Usually don't. Why should tonight be different?"

"Fibber. How did we get five kids?"

"Makes me wonder."

"You know they got here the old-fashioned way."

"Better show me. You said my memory is failing."

"Watch where you put your hands, fresh guy."

"You didn't mind when we were young."

"I didn't look like this back then."

"What's wrong with how you look?"

"A stranger stares back at me; an overweight, gray-haired old hag. I don't recognize her."

"Don't run yourself down."

"I no longer see curly brunette hair, or firm arms and a shapely waist in the mirror."

"Really? I hadn't noticed."

"I'm sorry. I wanted so much to stay young, for you."

"You're not old. You're two years younger than me."

"But I've gained forty pounds. Look at my hands; they're wrinkled as prunes. Lines in my face can route you to Phoenix."

"I'm no prize, either. Most of my hair has disappeared, my belt don't stretch around my stomach, and half my teeth are store bought."

"I miss my youth. The years are leaping by. Can't stop them."

"I don't mind Getting old, you know. What I regret is Being old."

"I remember Dad driving through Alabama when I was a child. Mountains in the distance looked blue. Think that's why they're called the Blue Ridge Mountains? Anyway, a peak in front of us looked as though it was moving away, even as we were getting closer."

"That's how I think of aging. Lots of years are zipping past. As I rack up more years, my perception of Old keeps receding, like that mountain peak."

"I think you've climbed the mountain, Harold."

"I've reached the top, for sure. I'm elderly, ancient, a senior citizen. You can call me all those euphemisms we use to avoid saying we're old."

"I think I looked okay when I was young. Maybe I was attractive, but I never was pretty. Boys told me I was cute, but they probably were laughing at me."

"Listen, Ms. Insecure. In the Navy, I traveled over half the world and met women in more than a dozen countries. After my hitch was up, I went through your drive-up lane at the bank. I couldn't believe my eyes."

"I remember. You stammered so badly, I couldn't understand you through the speaker."

"I looked through the bank window. You were the prettiest creature I had ever seen. You took my breath away. I could barely talk."

"I almost called the police, you mumbled so. I thought you were there to rob me."

"I'm glad you find it so funny."

"You did rob me, you know. You stole my heart."

"Mine stopped beating when I asked you for that first date. You're the reason I have a pacemaker."

"Before you turn out the light, hand me that telephone."

"It's late. Who are you calling?"

"Eye doctor, Hon."

"Office is closed."

"I'm leaving a voice mail."

"Why?"

"I'm cancelling your eye appointment. You see just fine."

FLOYD S. [STEVE] HULSEY

Steve Hulsey is a University of Florida graduate whose non-fiction articles and short stories have appeared in regional and national magazines. He is author of a published non-fiction book and has two novels and several short stories in progress. He and wife Sandra reside in Auburndale, Florida.

Next To Final Thrill

"That was some excursion. Don't you think so, Frank, dear?"

"One of the best, Marge."

"Too bad our cruise is ending and we have to return home."

"Know how you feel."

"It's time, though. Drink up. The ship's shuttle is here."

"Go ahead. I'm staying."

"How long? We're out of time."

"Maybe the rest of my life. That might not be long."

"You've drunk too many rum and Cokes again. Gosh, it's hot. Don't people in this part of the world believe in air conditioning?"

"Rum has nothing to do with it. I've thought this through very carefully."

"And you're staying? On this . . . this . . . pimple of an island? It's hundreds of miles from nowhere."

"Calm down. Read the travel brochure. Says we're in a tropical paradise."

"Frank, it's a hot, primitive slum."

"Quiet, peaceful, and unspoiled. Perfect place to live out my final days. Do you want a drink?"

"You can't stay here. We've collected responsibilities during forty-three years of marriage. We have a house. A car. Bills."

"They're expensive burdens."

"Friends. Relatives. For God's sake, Frank. We have a dog."

"You go home and dump all that junk. I'm staying here."

"Frank, you've lost your mind. Now, stop this nonsense. Let's board the shuttle before we're stranded in this humid hellhole."

"On the contrary. I'm thinking more clearly than ever."

"This is a juvenile fantasy fueled by sun and alcohol. I've enjoyed these past few days as much as you, but your pipe dreams must end."

"Marge, this is not a pipe dream. It's something I must do."

"We spend every vacation on some ridiculous activity you must do. Five years ago you had to race those dirty old cows after watching that movie."

"Bulls, Marge. They were bulls."

"Whatever. You slipped in that cow . . .er, bull, dung, twisted your ankle, and hobbled on crutches for a week."

"A minor mishap. Could have happened to anyone."

"Probably saved you from catching a horn in your backside. The following year, you rode a boat under Niagara Falls. Caught pneumonia and was out of work three weeks."

"How did I know it would get so cold in Buffalo? I had no control over a sudden cold front slamming the Great Lakes."

"Don't forget the year you insisted on leading a flock of whooping cranes from Wisconsin to Florida."

"Never forget that trip."

"You went up in an ultralight aircraft, dropped your GPS on the way to Florida, and wound up in New Mexico. We drove to Florida with a U-Haul truck stuffed with honking birds. My ears still hurt."

"Look on the bright side. They were well traveled cranes."

"Then, while we were in Florida, you decided you had to Bungee jump off the Sunshine Skyway bridge."

"Another couple of minutes and I could cross another adventure off my list."

"And cracked your skull! Have you forgotten the Bungee was too long and you would've hit the water? From that height, it's like diving onto a concrete slab. Thank God that gambling boat crew spotted you and called 911."

"That kid didn't measure the cord correctly. A college math major, and he can't read a tape measure."

"Frank, you could have died."

"That's what I'm trying to tell you. This excursion was my penultimate adventure."

"I don't understand."

⊠The next to final thrill. When the last one is done, my life is complete.⊠

"Isn't that your goal?"

"It was. Until now."

"What has changed?"

"I was excited at first. I had experienced everything I wanted. Not perfectly, but closely enough."

"Oh, good. I can use the rest. Waiter, a Mai Tai, please. To go."

"Suddenly, it hit me. I realized this is my next to last adventure. When my final thrill is completed, whatever it may be, my life is over. I'll die. I can't risk having that final experience."

"That's nonsense."

"Marge, when I returned from the war, I sat in a wheelchair on the hospital ship's deck steaming into Upper New York Bay. I had enemy lead in my hip, a cast on my leg, my arm in a sling, and Army doctors said my walking days were over."

"Obviously, they were wrong. You were a regular Fred Astaire last night."

"I could see nothing but thick fog and mist. Then, the Statue of Liberty emerged like an apparition hovering in midair, a green goddess rising from the sea. That was an incredible sight."

"I haven't seen tears in your eyes since our wedding."

"I get emotional when I remember that morning. Sighting the statue motivated me to overcome my wounds. I learned to walk again. I overcame my depression and vowed to experience everything I can before I die."

"Frank, you're right. That's an inspiring story. Tell you what. You stay here. I'll return home and get rid of all our encumbrances."

"Life will be much simpler without all that junk."

"I'll sell the house and book a cruise as quickly as I can."

"Send me your arrival date and time. I'll meet you on the pier."

"Oh, I'm not coming back to this oceanographic outpost."

"Where should I meet you?"

"Not necessary. I'm going to Hawaii, or Fiji, or Tahiti. One of those lush Gardens of Eden I've dreamed of visiting. And I'm taking the dog with me."

"You're abandoning me?"

"You'll be free of all encumbrances. You can live out your life in peace. Avoid that final thrill. Live forever."

"Marge, darling, I believe I'm inspired to make another new beginning."

"What now?"

"I already have a lifetime of memories. Drink up, Marge. Our shuttle is ready. We're going home. Together."

FLOYD S. [STEVE] HULSEY

Steve Hulsey is a University of Florida graduate whose non-fiction articles and short stories have appeared in regional and national magazines. He is author of a published non-fiction book and has two novels and several short stories in progress. He and wife Sandra reside in Auburndale, Florida.

Meeting Crow

"Hey, sweet thing, mind if I perch next to you?"

"Doesn't matter to me. It's a free forest."

"What's your name?"

"None of your business."

"I'd like to make it my business. Can I offer you a bug?"

"No, thank you. I can catch my own bugs."

"Of course you can. I was just warming you up for my display."

"I've already seen three displays this week."

"But, for you, I've got a great display. I'm full of awk."

"You'd have to show some serious awk to impress me."

"Oh, I got some awk, sweet thing. I got *lots* of awk!

"Not interested."

"What a shame. And I flew all the way over here because you were special."

"What kind of special?"

"Well, to start with, your feathers are just so... *fine.*"

"Here we go."

"That's not all. I was watching you yesterday. I saw you mob a hawk with your cute little friends. You can work up a big 'ole caw when you need to. I like that in a female."

"Yeah, well I saw you too. And, do you want to know what I like in a male?"

"A big, glossy crest?"

"No, I like a crow that doesn't hang at the back of the flock while the females do all the hawk-chasing."

"Maybe I didn't chase so hard because I was saving my strength...so I could chase a little something later."

"Chase what?"

"Why, you, sugarfeathers."

"I don't need to be chased. And don't call me sugarfeathers."

"Okay, okay. But what does a crow have to do to get you interested? Start a nest?"

"Maybe."

"Will you wait for me while I store up some twigs?"

"I'm here."

"Then, I'll be back. See you in a few flaps."

"Don't rush."

"Uh, hey there, mind if I perch?"

"Great, another one."

"Sorry I didn't hear you. Do you mind if I perch here? Or are you with the crow that just left?"

"No. I'm not with him."

"Then, may I?"

"Free forest."

"Pardon?"

"Nothing. You can perch here if you want."

"Thank you...May I offer you a bug?"

"Can't you do any better than that?"

"I'm not sure."

"What do you mean, you're not sure?"

"It's my first mating season. Can I start over?"

"You've got until the wind shifts."

"Okay. Sooo...pardon me, Ms. Bird, but I was wondering if you might be interested in building a stable nest with an old-fashioned crow?"

"Well, shut my beak, do you know anybody?"

"Very funny. But I'm serious about mating with a quality bird. I've been watching you for days. A lot of males have lit here and flown. You're picky."

"You're right."

"And I haven't seen you preen with anybody."

"Of course, not. I'm not that kind of crow."

"That's good. And, oh yeah, I saw you chase a hawk yesterday."

"And where were you?"

"I was flying back from the lake when I saw all the females give chase. You led the mob. And, hey, where were all the males, anyway?"

"Good question."

"Anyhow, by the time I caught up, you'd already run him off. I was impressed. Like I said, brains and agility are important to me. I'm a good defender, but I need to find a mate that can handle the nest while I'm out."

"So you think I'm smart?"

"Oh, yes! And from what I've heard, you'd build a great nest."

"Really? Where'd you hear that?"

"Crows squawk. I also heard you'd probably lay big eggs."

"Watch your beak."

"Sorry, I meant it as a compliment."

"I didn't take it as one."

"Like I said, I'm not good at approaching. What I meant was…I think you'd be a good nester, and not just another set of pretty feathers."

"You think I'm pretty?"

"Well, sure. But I figured you already knew that."

"Now, I'll take that as a compliment."

"I put off approaching you because, well, you're beautiful. And I know I'm not as good-looking as that last crow who perched here."

"Him? He was all wingspan."

"I don't have much of a wingspan…"

"Don't sell yourself short. You've got a nice wingspan."

"…I think it's because I didn't eat enough worms when I was a fledgling."

"I said that I think you have a nice wingspan."

"You did? I mean, you do?"

"Sure. You just need to smooth out your landing."

"I'll work on that. I'll make it perfect…but just for you."

"Nobody else?"

"Look, you're the only crow I want to nest with. I'll fly wherever you want me to fly. I'll hunt whatever you want me to hunt. I'd even steal a chicken egg for you."

"You'd do that for me?"

"In a heartbeat. If you want one, I'm on it!"

"You know, the farmer's got a gun."

"I know. And I don't care."

"You're crazy"

"You're worth it."

"I don't want your feathers on my conscience."

"Well, can I, at least, start with a bug?"

"Fine."

"I promise I'll get you a great bug. I'll be back in a flash."

"Hey, hold up."

"What?"

"Why don't we just skip the bug and get right to the display."

"Seriously?"

"Sure."

"Ms. Bird, I am honored."

"Don't overdo it."

"Okay. But really, thank you. I'll give it everything I got."

"All right, then, let's see that wingspan."

"I'm all yours."

VICTORIA HUMPHREY

Victoria Humphrey is a humor writer, speaker and recovering homemaker who just jumped out of an empty nest - and into her third life. She is writing her first book and blogs as "Moda, a Full-time Dispenser of Wisdom" at www.wisdomofmoda. wordpress.com.

Halloween In Cassadega

"May I hold a personal object of yours? That ring will be perfect."

"It's kind of tight—oh, it's off. Why do you need to hold my ring?"

"Objects important to you give off vibes that help me connect to your spiritual self just as the aura I see around you does."

"I have an aura?"

"Yes, it's giving off sparks of doubt, but not from you. From those who brought you here. Don't worry. We get a lot of doubters on Halloween in Cassadega."

"Is that why most readers are closed tonight? I heard many think doing readings on Halloween disgraces the legacy of spiritualists who settled Cassadega."

"That's true. I agree with them. I wouldn't read for a curiosity seeker tonight either, but you are not just a frivolous reveler. You have strong spiritual connections. I see clouds of purple in your aura, which shows your psychic awareness. Your strongest aura, though, is orange, bright orange."

"Orange? What does that mean?"

"It means you are constantly concerned with others' well being.

Uncross your legs!"

"My legs?"

"Yes, crossing your legs or your arms closes you off to spirits who would help you. Shhhh I'm hearing from your guide. She's a small woman, as small as you. She transitioned to the other world at a young age. Does the name " Charlotte " mean anything to you?"

" Charlotte ? No. I've never known anyone named Charlotte ."

"You have, and she is with you, protecting you."

"What's wrong?"

"Just a minute. Your guide is telling me you must be careful in automobiles. I see you in an accident with two older women. You are not driving, but . . . you must remember what I am telling you. You can avoid predetermined outcomes by your actions if you are aware. UNCROSS YOUR LEGS."

"I'm sorry."

"You must be open for me to read you. Relax. Do you have a question for me?"

"Yes, what do you see me doing ten years from now?"

"Do you write?"

"Yes."

"A strong feeling is coming through regarding writing and publishing. I see you at a table signing many books. Your spirit guide stands behind you."

"Wow, that is my dream, to publish a book. What else do you see?"

"Many good changes in your life in ten years as long as you connect to your inner spiritualism and listen to your spirit guide along the way. Uncross your arms, sit back, relax, and take deep breaths. Relax."

"Now I'm feeling relaxed, almost dizzy."

"Just go with that feeling . . . go with it . . .

". . .and I see you out west, in a house with lots of wood inside, in the mountains. You are in an upstairs room among high tree branches and you are writing. This is years in the future after you have become a successful author. Your future holds many joys as long as you are cautious and tune into your spirit guide along the way."

"Whoa, I feel woozy. Must be the shock of hearing such good news."

"Yes, that's probably it. You may have your ring back. Thank you for coming."

"That's it? Oh, okay. Thank you."

---✦---

"Good Lord! What were you doing in there for an hour?"

"An hour? More like thirty minutes, if that. I think I got cheated, Jim."

"No way. Look at your watch."

"Eleven ten? It can't be! I went in there about ten o'clock. Now I *am* feeling weird. I got dizzy during the reading. Next thing I remember was hearing her in the middle of a sentence. She also kept telling me to uncross my legs, to open up. Oh my God, do you think she hypnotized me?"

"You know these fortune tellers are quacks. She may have hypnotized you to get information. Did she tell you anything she shouldn't have known?"

"Not really. The spiritual guide she described sounded like my grandmother, though. She was small and did die very young, but her name was the same as mine, not Charlotte. I've never known anyone named Charlotte . She did know I like to write, told me I was going to be a successful author. I'd like to believe that, but she was so off on Charlotte , I can't take it seriously. Let's get out of Cassadega. Even though she was off the mark, I'm beginning to feel spooky about those lost thirty minutes."

---✦---

"Oh my gosh, Jim, I just spoke to Aunt Gussie. You know she's working on Daddy's family tree?"

"Yeah."

"My grandmother, the one I'm named for? Her middle name was Charlotte ."

"No kidding."

"You know what this means? That psychic wasn't a crackpot. I *will* go to that writer's conference in Tampa next week with Roz and Margaret. I'M GOING TO BE A WRITER!"

---✦---

"Our exit is coming up next. We three are going to have such fun at this conference. Margaret and I are honored to be attending with a real writer – according to your psychic."

"Don't forget, Roz, he also warned about her riding with two older women."

"Who are you calling old, Margaret?"

"LOOK OUT!"

BEDA KANTARJIAN

Beda Kantarjian has published short stories in print and online. Her story, "Caring for Lily," appeared in *FWA Collection #2 - Slices of Life*. Another will be published in fall 2011 by Spruce Mountain Press in an anthology. She participates in two critique groups. And is a co-coordinator of the FWA affiliated Seminole County Writers. Anhinga.wordpress.com

The King and
His Twenty-Three Subjects

"Oi! You there! What are you doing?"

"I'm walking. What's it look like I'm doing? Who are you? More to the point, *where* are you?"

"Look up. Oak tree. Big, forked branch. Hulloo!"

"I say! You can talk! What about these others? Can they talk, too?"

"Me subjects? Nah, they can't talk. I can talk on account of I'm their King. The Fairy King of this forest gifted all the animal kings with human speech. That was right nice of him, don't you think?"

"You're the king of the crows?"

"Blimey, no. I'm the king of this *tree*, just the king of this 'ere lot. All twenty-three of 'em. And technically, I'm a blackbird."

"I don't believe in fairies."

"Well, they 'aint got much to say about you, either. You didn't believe in talking birds a minute ago. What are you doing walking in the woods, anyway?"

"I'm thinking. I like to take walks and think about things."

"What's that funny lookin' thing on top of your head? Looks like a giant mushroom."

"It's a torque blanche."

"A turk what? What the bloody hell is it?"

"A *torque blanche!* It's a chef's hat. I'm from that yonder castle, where I serve the King of my people as head cook."

"I know where the castle is, you twit! Lost two of me mates there last month. There used to be twenty-six of us. Damned tragic."

"How'd you lose them?"

"Well, it's spring time, isn't it? The people throw all the windows in the castle open and a bird can't help his self. Me mate Reggie flew in the parlor window and helped himself to some of the Queen's bread. It looked delicious from where we were perched. All slathered up with honey. Queen went out for a second and in ol' Reg went. Didn't see the handmaid sweeping in the corner. She grabbed the broom handle and bashed him a good 'un! Poor Reg never knew what hit him."

"Gods! A bad business, that. But it serves him right. I'm up at two in the morning on baking day, wearing my fingers to the bone kneading dough and slaving in front of a hot oven. My hands are blistered for days. For the love of my Queen, and not for some thieving bird! I'm chuffed he got bashed. Humph!"

"Are you glad his missus and his two little 'uns went hungry that night?"

"Er...no, I suppose not. But honestly, what did he expect? The hand-maid would say 'Here poor Mr. Blackbird, you go on and have the Queen's toast. Cookie can always bake more!'"

"Well, you could, couldn't you? It's not like birds have dough and ovens to bake bread in. Say...what's that you've got there?"

"Where?"

"There. Sticking out of your apron."

"Oh...um...it's just a bit of rye I picked as I was walking through the fields."

"Looks more than just a bit to me. There's enough there for a good sized loaf, I'd wager. You got some nerve, Cookie, callin' us thieves."

"Ah, bugger it! My wages aren't enough for a rat to live on! I only pinch enough to get by."

"So do we."

"You're birds! You've got the whole world to pilfer. But never mind the rye in my pocket. What happened to your other mate? How did he die?"

"Die? He didn't die. Poor devil. He'd be better off if he were dead."

"Do tell."

"Well, about a week after Reg met his broomy fate, a bunch of us were flying around the keep. A servant girl—that nice-looking one that always wears black—sometimes she puts out leftovers for us."

"That'd be Betsy. She's one of them bloody weird goth girls."

"Whatever. She feeds us. And I love that gold ring she wears. You know we blackbirds like a bit o' shiny stuff."

"I thought that was magpies."

"Don't bring those brutes into it! As I was saying...the girl left us some crumbs scattered in the courtyard and there we were pecking our little beaks out, when your King comes out of his storeroom carrying a bag in his hand. Such a jingling! Now I told you we like shiny stuff, but my mate Oliver...there's nothin' he loves better than the sound of loose coins tinkling in a purse. He's mad for it!"

"Go on."

"So, Ollie hears the King's moneybag jangling and he goes spare. Hops right up to His Majesty like he's some friggin' pet canary. And the King? He's lovin' it. He laughs, and the manservant that's with him laughs, too. The King reaches into the bag and pulls out a pretty new sixpence. He leans over and practically shoves the thing under poor Oliver's nose. Then he wags it back and forth and there goes Ollie, hopping back and forth; poor gent can't take his eyes off the thing. He's hypnotized. He's so fixed on that coin, he's singing and dancing like some bloomin' court jester. Made me ill to watch."

"So what happened next?"

"Well, the King tossed down the coin in front of the poor bird. When Ollie went to snatch it up, the manservant threw a cloak over him! The King told the servant he meant to make a pet out of him. Poor Ollie!"

"That *is* dreadful!"

"'Aint it, though? What I wouldn't give to get in that castle and rescue good ol' Ollie."

"Hmmm...perhaps I can help you. It'll be tricky, but it just might work. There's a foreign novelty dish. I could bake you and your fellows here inside of a pie and then..."

"You what? You mean to cook us up? After I went and spilled my heart out like that?"

"Of course not. There's a way to do it that doesn't hurt you. When the pie is sliced open you fly out...unharmed."

"Is it magic?"

"Aye. It's culinary magic, it is."

"And we won't get roasted in that hot oven you were on about?"

"Upon my word, not one pinfeather will be scorched. When the King cuts the pie, you and your subjects fly out and cause as much commotion as you can. I'll run off to the King's private chambers and see if Oliver's being kept there. If so, I'll set him free. How's that?"

"It's effin' brilliant! We'll do it. I'd fancy having a King-to-King chat with His Majesty and taking a peck or two at his fat arse. I sure wouldn't mind having a go at Miss Betsy's nose-ring, either. I do like a bit o' shiny stuff!"

MARIA KELLY

Maria Kelly lives in Pinellas Park, Florida. She was first published in 2010 with her story "World Wide Web." When not writing weird speculative fiction, Maria engages in frenetic Twitter activity, drinks enough coffee to float an armada, and reads lots of books. Follow her on Twitter: @mkelly317.

Exactly

"Bella, come here."

"What's up, Grandma?"

"Look, I got hits, four of them."

"Hits? Oh, the dating service. Did you open them?"

"I'm too nervous. You do it."

"Not a chance. It's your love life."

"It's not a love life. It's a social opportunity."

"Whatever. Anyway, you'd better read about those old guys before they all die of old age."

"When did granddaughters become so irreverent?"

"Just being realistic, like you're always telling me to be."

"Okay, okay. Here's the first one. *Dear Irina, I⊠*"

"Irina? That's not your name."

"I know, but my yoga class says Irina is sexier than Jane."

"Sexy? Geez, you're a grandmother."

"Grandmothers can't be sexy?"

"Exactly."

"You know I hate that word, Bella. It sounds so smug."

"But it's true about grandmothers. They're not supposed to be sexy."

"It is absolutely <u>not</u> true. Sex is like reading. You can enjoy it forever. You may need bifocals to improve the process, but it's still pleasurable."

"Gross. Anyway, it must have not been so pleasurable with Grandpa. You dumped the poor old guy."

"I enjoyed sex with Grandpa all right. The problem was all the other women who enjoyed it with him too."

"That's why you made him move out?"

"Remember the trainer he hired to come to the house?"

"Her? She wasn't even pretty."

"And your piano teacher and the physical therapist who took care of your mom that last year and Mrs. Gunderson at the library and..."

"Stop. This is more than an innocent kid needs to know about her own grandfather. You going to finish reading that Irina thing?"

"*Dear Irina, I like your picture. You're really hot. When can we meet?*"

"Hot? Geez, delete him right now."

"Why? It's nice to be called hot. Look at his picture. He's not bad. Kind of..."

"O-o-o, he's got a comb-over. You can't believe anything he says."

"Because he has a comb-over?"

"Exactly."

"Let's put him on hold and look at the second one. *Dear Alicia...*"

"Alicia? What happened to Irina?"

"I'm experimenting. *Dear Alicia, We have a lot in common. I'm also an engineer and a free agent. No kids, no pets, no...*"

"No kids? You didn't tell him you are raising a granddaughter?"

"It didn't seem pertinent."

"So what does that make me? Inpertinent?"

"The word is impertinent. You might want to look it up. Now, let's see what else he says 'loves to travel, to take off at a moment's notice'. Hmm, that doesn't work too well for someone raising a grand-daughter, does it?"

"Exactly."

"Okay. Here's number three. *Dear Jane, You are a good and generous person to be raising your granddaughter, even making it sound like fun.*"

"That sounds better. Read the rest of it."

"*I completed a 10K race last weekend and ride a bike every day. I'm a decent guy. Would you like to meet?"*

"I think you should give him a shot, Grandma."

"Me too. Let's look at the last one. *Dear Jane, I lost my spouse fifteen months ago and am lonely. I have a small dog (non-shedding) and am a good cook. Like you, I am looking for companionship. Would love to meet you.* Okay, he's a keeper too. Dating world, here I come."

"Bella, you're still up. It's late for a school night."

"You said you'd be home by ten."

"It's only eleven."

"Exactly. Why didn't you call?"

"Hey, who's the parent around here?"

"Grandparent, not parent. Anyway, if I'd been an hour late, you'd be howling."

"You're right. I lost track of time. He was nice."

"And?"

"And remarkable. He's the one who ran the 10K race. Not so special except that he lost one arm and a leg in Viet Nam."

"Geez, he doesn't have all his parts?"

"He has the ones that matter. You'll get to meet him next week. I invited him for dinner."

"Maybe I don't want to meet him."

"We can make our special lasagna. It will be fun. You can invite Danny if you want."

"Danny? He's so last week."

"Hi, Gran. How was the guy with the non-shedder?"

"Interesting. He's the one who lost his spouse."

"So?"

"The spouse was named Frank."

"Frank? As in a guy?"

"Exactly."

"Hey, that's my word."

"Not anymore. George, that's his name, likes that I do yoga and have a garden."

"So?"

"So, I have two dates coming up. That's good isn't it?"

"Is it? One guy is missing his parts and the other one is gay. At least Grandpa was whole and we certainly know he was straight."

"Exactly."

 # KATE W. LESAR

Kate LeSar trained nonliterate midwives in Afghanistan, taught health care workers in Calcutta, and trudged through Moscow's snowy streets to find a hot plate for her 300 square foot apartment. She lives in Tampa, Florida with her husband and fellow traveler and their toy poodle who carries his own backpack.

Your Name Has Been Chosen

"Hello?"

"May I speak to the head of the household?"

"Speaking."

"Good evening."

"Who's calling?"

"My name is Perry. May I have a few moments of your time?"

"For?"

"Your name has been chosen to participate in product-launch demonstrations for your area."

"I'm cooking, but—"

"I'll be brief."

"Go on."

"Your participation in product demonstrations enters your name into a drawing to win a seven-day cruise to Bermuda . That's a *big* return for your small investment of time. Right?"

"Right, bu—"

"Our innovative product promises to simplify your life."

"What prod—"

"Thank you for asking."

"Hurry it up, Per—"

"Allow me to explain about—"

"Hell-ooo-o."

"—our product demonstrations."

"That's enou—"

"With your permission—"

"Stop now."

"—our marketing experts will—"

"Did you hear m—"

"—arrive at your home—"

"NO. UH-UH."

"—on Monday for your personal demonstration."

"Can't you hear?"

"Remember that trip to Bermuda I mentioned?"

"I *don't* care."

"You're one step closer to packing your bags."

"Pack *this*, Per—"

"To participate in our demonstrations, please *press* or *say one* now to agree."

"Do *what*?"

"Sorry, head of household. Your selection did not register."

"Head of house—"

"Please *press* or *say one* now to agree, or—"

"Awww—geez."

"—press *zero* to repeat this message."

Joan J. Levy

Levy is a public relations/marketing professional and freelance writer. Her articles have appeared in Central Florida magazines. She is a short story writer. Her short story, *Line-Dried Laundry* won a Florida Writers Association Royal Palm Literary Award in 2009. Two stories were finalists for the RPLA in 2010.

Knowledge

"What's up?"

"You're what's up."

"Ryan, my cell phone is about to run out of juice. And, I'm right in the middle of studying for a final. Environmental chemistry. Tomorrow afternoon at 1:00."

"Testy. Testy. I thought older sisters were supposed to give their younger siblings undivided attention 24/7."

"Ryan, I'm under the gun here. What do you want?"

"I waaant the editor position of *The Campus Voice Online* and, since Mr. Mattson's your Senior Advisor and just happens to be responsible for choosing the editor, you offered to feel him out. So..."

"Yeah. Yeah. Sorry. I talked with him this morning, after taking his grueling Contemporary Lit exam. I should have called you right away, but I had to start cramming. Dartmouth can turn around and reject my already-accepted application if I don't graduate with a 3.5 GPA. Anyway, back to Mr. Mattson. I believe you're in, but he was a bit vague."

"Clarify vague."

"Okay. He said something like, 'Ryan's a talented reporter and his article, *Today's Politics – Today's Economy* received more hits – you know, number of times someone viewed an article - than the number of kids we have in this high school. He's a top candidate, but he's got competition.' I asked who you're up against and he looked at me like I was a lunatic. Guess I'm totally out of the loop. I have no clue who he's talking about."

"Probably Bridget Duffy. One of her articles had around the same number of hits. She's from a big family – six brothers, one sister. I'm thinkin' they were all online, clicking away on her article every five minutes."

"Bridget Duffy. Ahhh, now I remember. She wrote *Climbing the Mountain.* About success and all the obstacles you have to face before you can achieve it. That piece totally rocked."

"My butt it rocked."

"You're jealous. She's smart and she's one hot chick."

"Whose side are you on anyway, Grace?"

"I'm always on your side, bro. Just telling you the way it is. She writes...almost as well as you do."

"Okay, she's good. Hot? Uh-uh."

"Oh my God! I completely forgot. Duh. You took her to the Junior Prom."

"That I did. And, lemme tell you, she's as cold as the freezing rain that assaulted us with ice pellets last December. When I walked her to the door, she shook my hand! Now who does that? Why are you laughing?"

"You're funny. Listen. Sounds like she played hard-to-get. That can be a good thing, Ryan. And, by *hot*, I meant pretty - with that long, charcoal-black hair down to her waist, milky-white skin, sapphire eyes. I'm guessing you invited her to the prom 'cause she's a looker and her brain circuits are fine tuned."

"Ryan, are you still there?"

"Yeah. I'm here." Why are you always right? Don't answer. I gotta go. Thanks for having the chat with Mr. M and good luck on your exam."

"You're welcome and I could use the luck. Later."

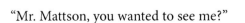

"Mr. Mattson, you wanted to see me?"

"Yes. Come in, Ryan, and take a seat."

"Uh...Bridget. How's it goin'?"

"Good, Ryan. How about you?"

"Not bad. Not too bad."

"Ahem. First of all, thanks for coming to my office on such short notice and I appreciate your willingness to meet with me on your day off. I'm sure you both wanted to sleep 'til noon. Everyone's wiped out after exams. I'm also sure that you're both anxious to hear who I've chosen to replace Thomas as editor of the school newspaper so I didn't think you'd mind sacrificing some sleep.

"Of the twelve reporters we currently have on the newspaper's staff, you two offer talent I haven't seen in the eight years that I've been *The Campus Voice Online*advisor. You each have a unique style. When you make a point, it's clear. When you provide information, it's factual. Your use of vocabulary is correct. And, I'd like to shake the hands of the teachers who taught you punctuation.

"Your knee is bouncing, Ryan. I imagine your brain is spinning as fast as the fan belt on that Ford Mustang of yours. Please bear with me. I'm getting to the point.

"Since September when you both joined the staff, you've run head-to-head in readership and the readership increased each month. Then in January – you saw the Reader/Hit Count Report - your political piece, Ryan, and your inspirational one, Bridget, showed an increase in readers by the thousands.

"Following that edition the Principal and I received emails and phone calls from students, teachers, parents and people not even affiliated with the school. They praised your creative skills.

"Why are you staring at me that way, Bridget?"

"I, I.., I am just so shocked. I mean I knew readership grew, but I thought kids were just clicking away for fun, distorting the statistics."

"Well, I think I just proved to you that's not the case."

"Yes. Yes, you did."

"Hmm. I kinda thought the same as Bridget. Guess I was wrong."

"Sometimes knowledge changes everything. As I gathered knowledge in order to make the decision you're waiting to hear, I realized a change needed to occur. You may not agree, but I believe the change is necessary for the paper to operate efficiently, especially due to its recent growth. As of today, *The Campus Voice Online* will have two editors - you two, if you accept.

"You're both smiling. I take that to mean you both accept. Next Wednesday, we'll meet again to sort out areas of expertise – News, Arts and Entertainment, Sports, Features, Student Life, Opinions, Polls, etc. and split them accordingly. Now, I'm late for my meeting with the principal."

"Wait. Please. Thank you, Mr. Mattson. Thank you very much!"

"You're welcome, Bridget. I look forward to working with you."

"You know what? This is awesome. Thanks. Thanks a lot, Mr. M."

"See you both next week."

◆

"So, Bridget, I'm thinkin' it would be a good idea if we went out Saturday night to discuss our new responsibilities."

"You mean, like, on a date?"

"That's what I'm talkin' about. Pick you up at 8:00?"

"Well, hmm... Okay. We do have a lot to discuss. See you at 8:00."

◆

"Hey Ry."

"Hey to you. Keep missin' you at home so I thought I'd call. How'd ya do on your exams?"

"Aced every single one."

"Congrats! Dartmouth, watch out, here she comes."

"I hope you follow me there. Anything happen yet with Mr. Mattson?"

"Grace, I got it. I'm editor! And...so is Bridget. I'm good with that, though. As a matter of fact, I have a date with her Saturday night."

"Sweet! I'm proud of you and maybe, just maybe, those ice pellets will melt."

LINDA MALLOY

Linda Malloy has one short story published in *FWA Collection #1 – From Our Family to Yours*. She is currently seeking to publish her children's chapter book, *Miss Snapperfin, Memories*, which won First Place in The Infinite Writer's *Do It! Write 2010 Literary Competition*, in the Middle Grade Children's Book category.

Bombs Away

"Grandpa, tell me what you did in the army. Did you shoot people?"

"No, I was in the Engineering Corp. We built things."

"Like what things?"

"Like roads, airfields, bridges. Those kinds of things."

"But Europe has roads and bridges."

"Yes, they do, and they did back then, too. Come sit by your Grandpa, and I'll explain."

"Okay."

"During the war, the Germans bombed the bridges and airfields so we couldn't use them. The Engineering Corp. went in and rebuilt them so the army could keep moving and airplanes could land."

"What was the biggest thing you ever built?"

"Well, the biggest thing we *almost* built was an airfield."

"What's an airfield and how come only almost?"

"An airfield's like an airport. A place where airplanes land. They'd come in, load more bombs and get more fuel and take off again. In those days, planes couldn't fly as far as they do now."

"That sounds simple. Pour a bunch of concrete, bring in fuel, and there you go."

"Yes, well, it wasn't that easy. We couldn't just call for a load of concrete. We had to make a smooth landing spot in the dirt. Plus we were in Germany in a very wooded, hilly area. We had to chop down trees, remove stumps, and flatten everything to make the runway."

"That still sounds easy to do."

"Sometimes it was. But sometimes it was hard. If the Germans found out what we were doing, they'd wait till we almost finished. Then they'd fly over at night and bomb our airfield."

"What a waste. Did you go somewhere else?"

"No, we filled in the holes and fixed the whole airfield. But on the day we were finishing, the Germans came by and bombed it again."

"Man, I bet you were pissed."

"That's an understatement and don't say 'pissed.'"

"Sorry. What did you do?"

"We decided to try something different. We faked our work on the airfield. We filled the holes with straw, making them look fixed when they weren't. Two miles away, though, under the cover of night, we built a real field. We covered that one with camouflage nets and we didn't use any heavy equipment. We did it all by hand. We thought we were smart, and we were sure we had fooled the Germans."

"Cool. You did a trick."

"Yes, but it wasn't tricky enough. The day before we finished the new field. We were pretending to work on the old fake field in the late afternoon, and a squad of German bombers came flying toward us. They lined themselves up to bomb the old fake one. We were ecstatic. We'd fooled them. Sure enough, they came streaking in and bombed the fake field. With cabbage. Pounds and pounds of cabbage splatted all over the fake field. All of us just stood there laughing our heads off. Within minutes another squad came flying by. This time with real bombs, and they blew up our real field."

"Did you build it again?"

"No, we gave up and moved onto a bridge that needed rebuilding."

"Why did they drop cabbage?"

"Because in the middle of a war, where both sides hate each other, it helps to just have a laugh. To know people are people. And bombing a field with cabbage was plain funny. You have never laughed so hard until you see how big a splat a head of cabbage makes. And the smell, whew. I often wonder if I went back there today, if that old landing strip would be growing cabbage."

Becky McGregor

Becky McGregor; wife, mother of four and grandmother of one. I was a Computer Science Engineer who wrote technical manuals and briefs. About the time I retired, my husband and I became the keeper of our family history and genealogy. I am now writing family stories and my memoir.

Beads on a String

"Grandma Becky, can I play with the beads?"

"Sure, Logan. I'll get the jar down, you go get a towel to put down on top of the table."

"Grandma, will you tell the story, please."

"You know the story. I've told it too many times to count."

"Tell me again. Please, please?"

"Okay, before you pour the beads out on the towel, remember they're very old. You have to play with them nicely or they'll break."

"How old are they?"

"Well, I don't know exactly. But they've been in our family for five generations. If I count you, it's six generations. The beads were a gift to your great-great-great-grandmother Mary Edna. All because she had a kind heart."

"No, no, you're telling it wrong. You have to start with the knock on the door."

"Okay, I'm the poor lady knocking."

"Knock, knock, knock."

"Now I'm Mary Edna."

"Yes, can I help you?"

"My name is Vy. I am in need of food, but I have nothing to trade, and I have no money. Anything you could spare would be appreciated greatly."

"I have some extra food and a few other items you might need. I'll bundle them up."

"Thank you. I'm much obliged."

"And her clothes were funny, her hair was wild, and she was a stranger. Right Grandma?"

"Yes, dear. She was a gypsy."

"But then the women came back and - - "

"Hey, who's telling this story? Look at the beads dear, and I'll finish the story. Yes, the women came back."

"Knock, knock, knock."

"Yes, can I do something else for you?"

"No, thank you, ma'am. You were so kind, I went back to our home and brought you some beads. They are strung together and form a curtain. You know, for a doorway. I placed a good luck spell on them. Keep them hung up, and you and yours will have good luck."

"You didn't have to do this. I had food to spare."

"I know, but this is a gift freely given. Thank you."

"Tell me what kind of good luck Mary Edna got from the beads, Grandma."

"From the day she hung the beads in the doorway to her bedroom, Mary Edna had good luck with her crops. She had more than enough food. She had so much more, soon other gypsys came to the house to get food from Mary Edna."

"How did you get the beads?"

"Well, Mary Edna gave the beads to her granddaughter Jo Ann when Jo Ann was seven years old. Unfortunately, Jo Ann's cousins took and destroyed about half of the beads. Since Jo Ann was so young, Jo Ann's mother Vickie hung them in her house to protect them."

"What kind of luck did Vickie have?"

"She had luck with true lifelong friends. Everyone loved Vickie and would do anything for her. No matter where Vickie went, she knew everyone. Then, when Joann got married, she took the beads with her."

"Did Vickie lose all her friends when Jo Ann took them?"

"No, the beads' good luck staid with Vickie, and her friends stayed with her for life. The beads gave good luck to Jo Ann. Jo Ann became lucky with money. Never a lot of money all at once, but small amounts here and there. Family and friends were amazed at how lucky Jo Ann was with money."

"Where did Jo Ann hang the beads?"

"Well, by that time, the strings started breaking and some of the beads fell off. So Jo Ann put the beads in this glass jar. But look at how the light still sparkles off them. See how every bead is unique. Different shape, different color, different texture, each bead made by hand by someone who tried to capture a rainbow in a bead."

"How did you get the beads Grandma?"

"In every generation, there's been one person who became enchanted with the beads and their story. One person who loved the beads. One who cherished them. So in that way, the beads themselves picked the person who received them next. That's why Jo Ann, my mom, your great-grandmother, gave them to me."

"How do I become enchanted? So I can get the beads."

"Sweetie, don't worry about it, because I think you already are. Now, carefully look through the beads and find the one with the flower painted on it. That's always been my favorite."

Becky McGregor

Becky McGregor; wife, mother of four and grandmother of one. I was a Computer Science Engineer who wrote technical manuals and briefs. About the time I retired, my husband and I became the keeper of our family history and genealogy. I am now writing family stories and my memoir.

License and Registration Please

"License and registration Ma'am."

"Have I done shomething wrong ofisher?

"You made a California stop back there, Ma'am. You do know you can't simply roll through a stop sign? You must come to a complete stop."

"Oh, ish that sho?" Well, you shee ofisher, I guess I mush have read the shine wrong. I went through a shtop shine? Oh dear. I'm shure my wallet's shomewhere in my pursh. Ah, oh, jush a sec. My pursh is kinda like the black hole. Ah,here tish."

"Thank you Ma'am. Your name is Connie Wolsey, is that correct?"

"Yesh, oh yesh, I'm Mrs. Connie Woozy. Why are you shmiling?"

"Please step out of your car Mrs. Wolsey?"

"Why?"

"I'd like you to walk a few steps for me."

"Oh! For crying ouch loud. Jush cuz' I'm a shenior shitzen doesn't mean I'm a party girl! Geesh!"

"Do you need help getting out of your car Mrs. Wolsey?"

"Oh shtop! You don't shee a walker or cane in thish car do you? How many shteps should I take young man?"

"Follow me please as I walk backwards a few steps."

"How's thish?"

"Very good Mrs. Wolsey. Have you been drinking any alcohol today Ma'am?"

"Of all the inshults! Ohhh wait. . .now I shee. Ish my mouth huh? My mouth is show numb right now. I jush left the dentish. Oh no! I don't beleesh thish. Aaack! Write me my tickesh quick! Pleesh hurry offisher!"

"What's the matter Ma'am? Are you feeling ill or something?"

"Don't be shilly offisher. I just glanshed at myshelf in the shide view mirror! You thought I wash shpeeding my way to Clown Alley didn't sha?"

"Well ah, no Ma'mam, heh, not at all."

"You laughing ash me young man?"

"I'm sorry Ma'am, but I ah, can't help it."

"Well I'll be! Woosh you take a bit of sherious advishe from this ol' lady, offisher?"

"Yes, Ma'am."

"Now you lishen closhly. Don't ever, ever, put lipsthick on your lips right after you get your mouth numbed up at the dentish. She what happens?"

"I do Mrs. Woolsey. Well, consider this a first and only warning Ma'am. Next time I'll give you a traffic ticket if I see you rolling through a stop sign."

"Oh, thank you offisher. You da' besht. Poooosh."

"What?"

"Shmile young man, I wash jush trying ta blow you a kish ."

CLAUDETTE PARMENTER

Claudette Parmenter: Published Columnist, Ghostwriter/Author of published WWII novel titled, *Twin Destinies*. Has previously published in secular, Christian and military publications throughout her freelance writing career. Winner of 2004 FWA's Royal Palm Literary Awards, Unpublished Novels, Romance category - *Rice and Roses*. Currently a Writers Group Leader for FWA.

Beer and Mary Beth

"Hey, how ya doin'?"

"Fine. Washington High? Whoa! How long's it been – eight years?"

"Yeah. Whatcha been up to?"

"Just home visiting the folks. I live in Florida now."

"Really? That's cool. What's goin' on down there?"

"Nothing much. The summers are hot, so we get away for a couple weeks. Not that it's much cooler here—it must be 95 today."

"Yeah, the dog days are comin' earlier now. July instead of August."

"Oh yeah. I remember August: no air conditioning. Windows would be wide open at night but we'd still sweat in bed."

"So how you keepin' busy down there?"

"I'm working in a machine shop. Got a degree in mechanical engineering and now I design parts. You heard of CAD and CAM programs?"

"Can't say I have."

"Oh. Well, so, what are you up to?"

"Still hanging here. Me and Mary Beth got married."

"Wow, congrats, man. When did that happen?"

"Seven years ago. Got three kids. Manage the little grocery out on Barker Road."

"Three kids? Man, you've been—how is Mary Beth? I haven't talked to her since, forever. I mean, before you two were going out, I think."

"She's doing great. Stay at home mom. Real good cook. Takes care of us."

"All boys?"

"Oh yeah. Hunnert percent."

"I always wondered what happened with you guys. You were quite the couple senior year. Never saw anything on the alumni mailings, though."

"Yeah, well, we don't go in for that much."

"Understood."

"Just not our thing."

"Uh-huh. So. The grocery store."

"Yep. Manager."

"That's great."

"Pays the bills. Plus it's air conditioned."

"Barker Road. Isn't that where we got beer our sophomore year?"

"The same."

"Barker Road beer runs. I remember them like they were yesterday."

"Yep."

"You, me, Mary Beth, The Rog, J. C., little Lily What's-her-name. Fake IDs and keep your head down. Drinking out on Carpenter Road."

"Mary Beth?"

"Your dad ran the place then, didn't he? You take over for him?"

"No, he's still there. But I don't think I remember Mary Beth coming with us."

"You don't? She always hung out with Lily. Still can't remember her last name. Starpen-something or other; it was a long one. I think she moved the summer before senior year."

"Oh, that Lily. Yeah, her last name was too hard for me to say. She was a foreigner."

"German, I think. But not all stiff like the stereotype, that's for sure. Wild and fun to be with, just like Mar—so, when did you and Mary Beth start going together, September?"

"Yeah. Never got up the nerve before that. Wished I had. We're like two of a kind."

"Start of Senior Year."

"Yeah. She had just gotten out of a bad one. Don't remember who with—she wouldn't say—I shouldn'ta told her I'd kill the guy. I wouldn't, but I woulda beat the crap out of him if I'd found out."

"I have no doubt."

"But me and Mary Beth, it was like we were made for each other. Soul mates, ya know?"

"Yeah, sounds great. Well, it was nice running into you. Tell Mary Beth I said hi."

"Will do, thanks. But, I gotta ask ya one thing."

"What's that?"

"It's kinda embarrassing, but, ya know, I just can't remember. What's your name again?"

John Rehg

John Rehg resumed writing five years ago after a hiatus of over 25 years. He has published a collection of spiritual reflections, several short stories, and is working on revising his first novel. John leads the St. Petersburg chapter of the FWA. Please visit http://www.johnrehg.com.

A Muse Paper

"This one's as dim as a bologna sandwich."

"Relax, Papyrus. You've been doing this work for centuries and you know how difficult humans can be. If she's serious about writing, you'll find a way to break through."

"I send her the plot, she turns on the TV. I send her a commercial with the perfect opening line, she washes the dishes. If she'd sit still for half a second I could download the entire story. She's incapable of paying attention."

"Who said being a writing muse for everyone on earth would be easy? It seems there's not one soul down there, except for maybe that adorable insurance gecko, who hasn't thought about writing a book. Why not focus on the ones you've already helped?"

"Because, for every successful writer, there are millions who never get to see their work in print. Even the gecko will imagine himself an author one day. I'm just plain tired, Pleiades."

"It's impossible to reach them all."

"Why couldn't I have inherited my sister's job? Come on, a music muse? All she has to do is send a few melodic repetitions and toes start tapping. The rest is sheet music history."

"Calliope has her problems, too. Look at what happened after she introduced heavy metal."

"Definitely a wrong note."

"Take a deep breath and concentrate on the writers who already understand the process. There's always little Stevie."

"Oooh, how I love that man. He picks up everything I send. It's like we're having a real conversation. I make his car stall and he pens *Christine*. After the St. Bernard incident, as soon as the bandages came off, *Cujo* was born. I'm thinking about delivering him my shopping list next week. If he could type faster, I'd give him every story I've ever created and retire early. But, for every Stephen King, there are so many more who don't get it. Like that annoying Margaret Mitchell."

"She was an odd bird."

"I channeled her one of my all-time favorite novels. I then made the attempt to send her, *Atlanta Storm*, the perfect title for the book. She was outside hanging laundry when I began to generate turbulent weather. Unfortunately, some clothes flew off the line and Margaret lost a few of her unmentionables. The next thing you know she created her own title for the book. I did my best to inspire. She betrayed me. Frankly, I was so annoyed I never sent her another damn word."

"Still, that one turned out to be a classic. It's your gift to reach an artist's soul, even if parts get lost in the translation. Look how long it was before you got through to Hemingway."

"He was a tough nut to crack. It took a while to realize he needed a few drinks before he could receive my material. Then, due to his relaxed state, I had to send him simple sentences, one at a time. Took forever."

"You'll figure out a way to connect with this new writer, too. What's her name, Barbara something?"

"Yeah, Barbara. Don't hold your breath."

"You can do it. Just, please don't send her any ideas while she's taking a shower. I don't want a repeat of the Charlotte Brontë incident."

"Water through the drain. Let it go."

"Papyrus, I've got an idea. Why not tell this new writer about your life? If she could understand how the writing process actually works, she'd sprint to the computer."

"Sure, Pleiades, I'll just send her information about a muse who smacks his head against the wall in an attempt to send out stories. A muse who floats ideas ripe for the picking to ungrateful people who profess their love of the craft, but refuse to spend time putting words on paper."

"What have you got to lose? If she does get the gist and publishes the story, you may actually get a little credit for your brilliant mind."

"And I the master of your charms the close contriver of all harms, was never called to bear my part, or show the glory of our art . . ."

"I hate it when you quote yourself."

"You know I am sick of authors saying their ideas simply come to them out of the blue. It would be great, after all these years, to receive at least one thank you. Worth a try, Pleiades. What would I do without you, my little star?"

"That's my muse. Try one more time to get her attention. Don't take long though, dinner's almost ready."

"Wait, do you think it's too harsh to tell her writers are not as smart as they think they are? That it's my ideas they're gathering and if they don't act quickly someone else will grab them first. And . . . What's Barbara doing now? Dear gods, she's watching *The Housewives of New Jersey*. She's never, ever going to make it as a writer. That's it, I'm done for today. Let's eat. What are we having?"

"Fried bologna."

"Funny. I'll take mine with a scotch."

"Worked for Hemingway."

BARBARA SAMUELS

Barbara Samuels is an award-winning humor writer from the Treasure Coast. She is an active member of the Morningside Writing Group and the Palm City Word Weavers. Currently she is editing her first book, a collection of humorous essays entitled, *Grande Coffee and a Blueberry Scone.*

Passing Conversation

"Aileen, congratulations. I hear you're going to have a baby. Tell me, what name did you pick out?"

"We were thinking of Joshua David if it's a boy, and …"

"If? What do you mean if? Don't you know?'

"Of course not."

"But you came to the gene center."

"Yes, and I left right away. I felt uncomfortable when the doctor started talking about custom gene splicing. As long as the baby's healthy I see no need to tamper with nature."

"You can't be serious! Custom genetics isn't tampering. You're polishing out all the little imperfections that you won't have to put up later. Suppose you have a brown haired girl when you really wanted a blond boy? You'll never forgive yourself for not taking advantage of the science."

"I don't know, Denise. Pre-programming a child? It sounds so sterile, so clinical."

"So economical and necessary. Children need an advantage these days. Competition for jobs is so fierce. Think of the difficulty you're putting your baby in. He could start off stupid and stay that way.

"Oh, what a horrible thing to say."

"Well, it's true. Wake up, girl. It's twenty fifteen. We not only don't have to have children, we can have exactly the child we always wanted. There's nothing maniacal about reprogramming genes to correct catastrophic disease, is there?"

"No, I guess not."

"So why is it wrong to correct for physical appearance and abilities? Think of it this way. If your son already has the build and stamina for sports, then he won't need to shoot up steroids to compete. You're only hindering your baby's potential with your backward thinking."

"Oh, you are so horrible. Children are a gift from God. I should think He knows what he's doing."

"I am so sorry that you feel that way. I can't change your mind?"

"No, not with such ugly arguments."

"Have it your way. Control, this is Agent Four, sector nineteen. Send in the bus."

"You're wired? Who are you talking to?"

" Don't struggle, Aileen. You're under arrest."

"What? What? Who are you?"

"I'm a government agent, Department of Child Services. You refused to take advantage of the best medical services for your child. We deem you unfit for motherhood. How can we build a strong, dominant society if people continue bearing defective children willy nilly?"

"You can't do this. I have rights. What kind of bus is that? It looks like a mobile hospital. Oh my God, you're not. Denise, please."

"Try not to bruise her, guys. She's just ignorant. I'll follow up at the end of my shift."

"No. No, let go of me. You're hurting me. You can't do this."

"I hate it when they get self-righteous after the fact. If people would just understand we're doing this for their benefit. Who's next?"

"So, Tamara, I hear you're going to have a baby."

Patricia Semler

Patricia Semler is an award-winning screenwriter, currently working on a television action pilot thru a Fellowship with the Writer's Boot Camp. A native New Yorker transplanted to Florida for the weather, Patricia finds time for needlework and gardening, as well as tackling the short story format.

THE ULTIMATE CRITIQUER

"Hello, Mother. Good of you to call so late."

"W e l l l l…how did it go?"

"It didn't. You were right. I should have let you read it first."

"Mmmm…what happened?"

"They just didn't get it…oh, a couple of them thought it was pretty good, but most actually took offense. And Mother, however bad my writing is, I would never intentionally offend. You know, in writing groups we're always told not to take it personally."

"I know that, dear, but you have a way, sometimes, of unintentionally saying the wrong thing. I don't mean to offend, Kit, but your sense of humor is a little weird at times."

"Yes, Mother. Thank's for your support. I'm going to get a snack now and watch some TV. I'll talk to you tomorrow."

"I'm coming over."

"Mother, it's after 9 o'clock."

"You always stay up late, and you know I do, too. I'll be there in fifteen minutes, but don't unlock your door until you're sure it's me. You can never be too careful."

"Mother, please don't..."

✦

"Let me see it."

"Mother, just sit down and I'll fix you a cup of tea, but..."

"Let me see it."

"Mother, really...okay, if you have to...here. Sit and make yourself comfortable. You know, it was just supposed to be a kidding, kind of caricature of their writing, but definitely not insulting. I..."

"Quiet, I'm reading. Oh, no!"

"What's wrong? Your heart, Mother! Are you all right?"

"Tenure...tenure. Kit, you can never, ever, kid about tenure. With your father and me both being teachers, how could you not know that?"

"It was a story thing. It wasn't meant to be real."

"It's real to a teacher, dear. Your father and I held our breaths every year until we got tenure. You can't kid about something that serious."

"I'm sorry. I didn't mean it like that."

"Hush, I haven't finished."

"Okay, Mother. What's the verdict?"

"I'm glad to see that you learned to punctuate reasonably well, and your spelling is generally good. Your sentence structures are adequate. Now, about the content..."

"The content...of course."

"I know that you are a good person with a kind heart. Unfortunately, you inherited your father's impulsive brusqueness, and his exaggerated, warped sense of humor. I can see that you thought this was fun, and it probably was...in your head. Your mistake was putting it on paper. However, when it was still just in your head, what did you want it to say?"

"I wanted to say that it's fun being a part of this group and walking through their worlds of imagination. I could never write about things like believable space persons, or vampires, or...or...all the things they create stories about. I really don't know where all their ideas come from."

"But tenure, Kit. What made you pick on such a subject?"

"I would have no idea how to write an interesting story about tenure. That takes a ton of creativity. So I thought I would try parroting one that someone else wrote, and it was fun...at least for me...but apparently not for the others. I blew it."

"You did, but it's not the end of the world, daughter. It is, however, a very important learning experience...what you might call a failure to communicate. Even I, at 86, am not too old to learn, so you certainly aren't. Next time you write something, call me to critique it before you submit. Now, have a small glass of wine, soak in a warm bath, and get a good night's sleep. I'll come by to have lunch with you tomorrow and we can talk some more about tenure."

"What an idea, Mother."

"Night, dear. Make sure your doors are locked."

◆

"Mornin' love. Judging by the amount of wine gone from this bottle, I'd say you had a darn good night's sleep."

"Ohhhh, Stan, don't talk so loud."

"Here, Kit, drink some coffee. It'll help. Was your critique that bad?"

"Not just the group. My mother came by to add her two...or twenty cents' worth."

"Uh oh! I should've stayed up."

"Wouldn't have made any difference. When Mother is on a mission..."

"How bad was it with your mom?"

"Oh, it put me back in grade school."

"You let your mother do that to you all the time."

"Yeah, I hate that. She was a teacher, not a writer. What does she know about critiquing? It galls me. She thinks she's always right."

"Was she right about your submission?"

"Yes, dammit!"

"Are you going to let her read the next one before you submit it?"

"Yes, dammit!"

FAUN JOYCE SENATRO

I'm a retired Social Worker and late blooming aspiring author. I live in Port Orange with my husband of forever and our miniature daschound, Noli (Go, Seminoles!). Priorities are our kids (nine), grandkids (nineteen), great-grands (twelve) and the dog. I volunteer, walk, read and write.

Two Donuts
and One Rut to Go

"Okay, Madge, let's take this booth, our coffee and donuts will be here in a minute. You gonna bring your Chocolate Cherry Surprise Cake to the annual church Bake Off and Bake Sale?"

"We always take this booth, Ellie. It's like the Happy Coffee Cup reserves it for us every Tuesday."

"What about your Chocolate Cherry Surprise Cake, you're gonna enter it aren't you?"

"I don't think so."

"What? You always enter your Chocolate Cherry Surprise Cake. It's won a ribbon for years. And, it sells five minutes after the prizes are announced."

"I don't know, Ellie. You gonna bring your Blonde Brownies? Oh, here comes our girl with the coffee and donuts. Thanks."

"I always bring my Blonde Brownies, Madge, you know that. They're popular, too, you know. Not everyone likes chocolate. Not that your cake isn't always a best seller and a real winner, like I said."

"I thought maybe, *if* I bring anything, I'd bring something different this year."

"Like what? Honestly, Madge, I don't understand you. Why something different? Your Chocolate Cherry Surprise Cake is a sure winner. And, you not bring anything? I can't believe that."

"Last year my Chocolate Cherry Surprise Cake took third."

"Well, you can't take first place every year."

"I know but maybe with something different...different sounds good to me right now."

"Different sounds good to you? What the heck does that mean?"

"It means maybe I'm tired of doing the same things over and over again. What's wrong with something different? God forbid, even exciting?"

"Now I am worried about you. Exciting? Madge, what're you gonna do that's exciting? Bake a coconut cake?"

"I don't know. Maybe I won't bake any cake this year."

"I don't believe that. Not for a minute. Why Madge you've been in every Bake Off and Bake Sale the church has had. I can't remember a year when you didn't enter. True, some of the first entries didn't get the...umm, recognition they deserved but when you found the recipe for that- Chocolate Cherry Surprise Cake, well, it took off. You're known for that cake."

"Ellie, I'm also known for bingo on Monday, bridge on Wednesday and hospital volunteering every Friday. Nothing changes."

"You have a good life; even after Harry passed you just kept to your routine. Your life is good, Madge. Why change now?"

"I know it's a good life and I'm not complaining. It's just...well, it's so monotonous. I mean here it is Tuesday morning and we're at the Happy Coffee Cup eating one French cruller apiece and having one and a half cups of decaf coffee. We don't even order a different kind of donut."

"You're bored with me; and you can order any darned kind of donut you want. I thought you liked French crullers."

"I do and of course I'm not bored with you. I didn't say that and I sure don't mean it Ellie. It's just that I'm gonna be seventy in three months and maybe it's too late to make changes. Stop pouting, I'm sorry if it sounded like I was tired of you."

"Well, it did sound like it. Where's that girl with the hot coffee. Mine's down to half already."

"There! Ellie, you even think the girl with the coffee pot should be in on our routines."

"Now that's silly, but she knows after we drink half our coffee we want a top up. We're here every Tuesday…"

"See. Even you have to admit we're in a rut."

"Well, what do you suggest will get us out of this rut? I kinda thought it was a comfortable rut. I like spending time with you. We have a lot in common, bingo, bridge, book club…oh, I see."

"Oh, Lord! If it's Tuesday it has to be Belgium ."

"What the heck does that mean?"

"It's an old movie."

"Did we see it together?"

"I don't think so."

"Okay, what do you think would get us out of this rut you seem to think we're in?"

"That's the problem. Maybe we've dug ourselves in so deep we won't ever get out."

"Now that doesn't sound like you. If you want out we'll do it together…that's if it's okay with you."

"Now don't go getting in a huff. Of course, if we change anything it would be together. You're my best buddy."

"Whew. For a minute I thought I was getting the old heave-ho."

"Think, Madge. Name something, just one thing you've always wanted to do but never got to. What would you like to do?"

"Well…I've always wanted to go on a cruise."

"A cruise? I'd never thought you'd say that."

"Why? I've had my dreams you know. I just don't talk about them."

"Me too."

"Me too what?"

"Dreams, I've never put this dream into words."

"Well, come on, I told you one of my dreams, you have to tell me one of yours."

"I think…I think we're too much alike, Madge.

"What's that mean?"

"Because…I've always wanted to go on a cruise, too."

"No!"

"Yes!"

"Drink your coffee, Ellie. We're gonna stop at that new travel agency at the Circle City Mall before we go home. We're comin' home with cruise tickets."

"And shop for cruise clothes?"

"Yes, and have lunch at that new tea room."

"Eat out twice in one day?"

"You wanted change? You wanted out of this rut? Well, hold onto your hat, lady, we're doing things different. It's all aboard for two old broads who are making changes. Here, let me get this check."

"That's different, too."

"Your fault. I guess they'll have to do without Blonde Brownies and Chocolate Cherry Surprise Cake this year."

"Hey, wrap your donut in a napkin. We'll eat them on the way to the Mall.

"Another change in our routine. Bye, bye rut."

 ## Sonia [Sunny] Serafino

Sunny Serafino, recognized for her ability to inspire readers with stories of courageous women, has published ten novels and a humorous memoir. Three novels have won literary awards. She also teaches creative writing at SFCC. Sunny Serafino lives in Avon Park, Florida with her husband Len.

Check out —www.sunnyserafino.com

Tilt

"What? You're not dressed yet? You'll be late."

"I know…but…"

"You're not changing your mind, are you? We decided."

"When I thought about being a parent, I never conjured this."

"Me either. I wonder: have I failed as a father?"

"It's not our fault or his. He's exceptional in so many ways; even his problems are off the charts."

"He was such a happy little kid. How did we get to this point?"

"What on our knees—literally and figuratively?"

"Yes. We've been living in this pinball machine of emotions and finally hit "tilt"."

"I wish you'd come with us."

"I have to work. Now, more than ever, we need the insurance. You'd better hurry."

"I can't decide what to wear. Getting dressed is the final domino that triggers everything; if I don't dress, the plan won't tumble into place."

"And we continue to run the hamster wheel."

"I know. Backing down is not an option. What I don't know is how to dress for this occasion. Does today calls for black? It feels a bit like a grieving moment."

"It's not his funeral. Don't make it worse."

"I'm taking my thirteen-year-old to be committed—certified as mentally unstable. Isn't that a death of sorts?"

"Mother, there's no need to exaggerate. Melodrama doesn't help."

"I hate it when you do that—dismiss my emotions like I'm a toddler throwing a tantrum. Once we do this, they'll be no going back. Medical records follow you forever nowadays."

"We've been over this."

"I just wish we didn't have to do it, you know?"

"But, we must. Stop crying; you'll frighten him. Think how desperate he must feel inside—hurting enough that he agreed to this."

"That's another crazy thing—that he has to agree. We're bringing him to the hospital because he's mentally unbalanced, completely out of control. The laws require his approval? Plus, He's just a kid; how does that make sense?"

"It is what it is and you can't avoid it by standing there in your bra and panties. Pull yourself together. You're a wonderful mom. He knows it. Finish dressing."

"I'll wear my flamingo necklace. He always comments when I wear it. He gave me the matching earrings for Christmas."

"Slacks and a shirt might be wise; otherwise they might offer you the group rate."

"I don't want to chance that; I'm too close to the edge."

"About the rest of your wardrobe...?

"I guess...gray pants...white blouse—everything else in my closet feels too cheery, almost manic."

"That'll work. It's subtle."

"Perfect camouflage for an extraordinary day."

"Call me when it's done."

"I feel like a hit man getting instructions from the Godfather."

"We're trying to put his life back on track, not end it."

"I want to believe this'll be the first step towards a solution. Wish I was more convinced."

"At least we're doing something. Otherwise it's like we've already given up on him. They'll get his meds balanced, experience what we've been facing 24/7 and provide us a better coping strategy."

"Pass me my perfume bottle, would you? Maybe Shalimar will cover the stink of fear I'm oozing…I remember spritzing it on his crib mattress so he'd have the comfort of my smell through the night."

"Always sounded like New Age mumbo-jumbo to me."

"For those of us whose noses function properly, smell is a channel that tunes in memory and emotion."

"I have this client—when she visits my office, I'm reminded of you. She's tall and beefy, so it's not her appearance; maybe it's her fragrance. Shalimar."

"It's like a grace note I carry with me into my day—for me."

"Today calls for every resource you can muster. Game on, for sure.

"Most moms take their kids to tee-ball and soccer. Not me. I take ours to the shrink. For us, the Big League isn't the state championships; it's the mental hospital…"

"There you go being maudlin again."

"Easy for you to say; you're on your way to work. I'm the one executing our plan…."

"I'm doing my part too."

"God, dropping him off for his first day at pre-school was hard. Where will I get the strength to leave him locked up in the psych ward—if they admit him?"

"We both know there's no if here. The boy needs help—professional help."

"Damn. These buttons are awkward."

"Here, let me do it.

"Really?"

"I meant the buttons."

"Yeah. I figured. I'm as ready as I'll ever be."

"Call me."

◆

"I'm glad to hear from you. What took so damn long?"

"It's not like going to the movies where anybody that pays is admitted. They want to be sure it's appropriate for the child."

"So?"

"No surprise; the doctor concurred with our assessment. She said when a child takes as many meds as he does, balancing them is challenging. Add the complication of adolescence, and you've got the perfect storm of irrational behavior."

"Perfect storm? More like World War III."

"Now who's getting dramatic?"

"Anyway, how did Dan react?"

"He was uncharacteristically calm, almost numb. I think he was relieved too, like he saw a sliver of hope on the horizon."

"Poor kid."

"I kissed him good-bye, gave him a hug and he left with a nurse. As he passed through the door, he turned and waved. His eyes were moist. He said nothing, just nodded his chin and allowed the door to close behind him. It locked shut with a loud thud."

"He put up a brave front, huh?"

"Nothing as macho as that. I think he was just resigned. And tired."

"I know I am."

"Me too. I feel relieved...guilty...terrified and hopeful at the same time."

"I guess that's parenthood."

"Nana used to say, 'Being a mom is the hardest job you'll ever love and would never quit.'"

"She got the hardest part right."

"The never quit part too."

"Never."

GAYLE SWIFT

For Gayle, the road of life has included bumps, twists and the occasional pothole. Writing provides an outlet and a way to reach others and create community. Her experiences as a teacher, business woman, adoption coach, mother and cancer survivor all fuel her writing energies and provide stories to share

Information, Please

"You can do the house inspection without me, can't you? I need to finish in the kitchen."

"Actually, ma'am, I need you to do the walk through with me. Don't worry. I'll be outa here in three or four minutes. Company policy and all that stuff. Companies today. They're all about protecting themselves. I can remember when you could go off and leave the neighborhood plumber all afternoon in your house to fix the broken toilet while you went to your kid's baseball game. Shoot, my mom left one time and my brother and me didn't even know where she was. We had some guys painting our house. Remember those old clapboard houses before all the fancy new sidings we have today? Well, my brother and me were too young to paint and my dad sure wasn't gonna do it. So these painters were about half way through when my brother and me climbed up on the roof and my brother no sooner got up there, when he slipped and fell. Fell off the darn roof and broke his arm. Ya' should 'a seen the expression on those painters' faces. One of 'em took us to the hospital …my brother wouldn't go without me, and the other guy stayed home waiting for Mom. I don't know which one was more upset, the one who took us to the hospital or the one who had to wait for Mom."

"Wow. Hmm. Ah, that's the living room right ahead. I don't know what ..."

"Nice room .That's quite a view of the lake. Any fish? I used to fish every chance I could. When I was a kid. Used to skip school. I actually got a 22 inch trout in a lake not far from here. When I was in college, I worked for the county a couple of summers stocking lakes. Must 'a stocked fifteen of 'em. Not just trout. We stocked a couple different kinds of bass, some crappie. Good job. Not much money but outdoors all day long. Afternoon swim whenever we wanted to. Bass are a lot easier to catch than the trout. I went bass fishing up north with one of those big time fishermen. One of his rods cost over $10,000. Made his livin' fishing. Think that might take the fun out of it for me though.You fish?"

"No. It's a little too hot and buggy for my ..."

"I'm used to the heat. Ya' think this is hot? My family had a farm in Texas . Now that's hot. Everybody has a couple of acres in Texas . Leading state in this country for number of farms and farm owners, and my daddy liked owning land. We even had a horse 'cause if you have a farm in Texas , you have a horse on it. We just had a pony, but it might as well've been a full grown horse. I could ride him, but he was a handful for everybody else. One time my dad took hold of him but backed him into the barbed wire fence. They got into a big 'ole fight. Daddy pulled on the reins and that pony left go with a kick to Daddy's back that put him on the ground first and the doctor's office next. Good thing we had mom around to stop him 'cause he was fixing to shoot that horse as soon as he finished paying the doctor's bill.

"I guess it's hard to be a farmer with a bad back. I'll show you upstairs."

"You're right about that. Ended up here in Florida with a little place just below Disney World. We had grapefruit trees, orange orchard, but our best crop was avocados. You wouldn't believe how big our avocados were. Big as my head. People think of California when it comes to avocados, but southern Florida grows some whoppers. Actually I think I saw some even bigger in the Disney greenhouses. Disney has all kinds of farms, It's not just an amusement park. They breed cattle. Do all kinds of horticulture. They grow a lot of the vegetables and most of the herbs that they use in their restaurants. In fact, the biggest tomato I ever saw was at Disney. Was hanging from one of those upside down baskets. This area out here where you live used to be the nation's largest producer of celery. It's all sand, but celery can take sand."

"I didn't know that. This way to the family room. It's a bit of a war zone. Probably mud all over the place, but ..."

"War zone and mud huh? I know all about both. I did a couple of tours in Iraq. Talk about mud. And if you want to talk about the true definition of what hot is, ain't no place hotter than Iraq. The Army has air-conditioned jeeps. Problem is, Iraq's nothing but mud in most places. My buddy and me were auto mechanics over there and most of the time we spent cleanin' the mud off the air-conditioning coils so that the air would work in the jeeps. We figured a way to prevent the build-up. Designed a screen to put in front of the coils and bingo! No more mud on the coils. Too bad we belonged to Uncle Sam at the time. Could've made lots of money if we'd been civilians. Solve a problem while you're in the military and the idea belongs to the government. You don't get a penny or your name on the patent. Just a commendation from your commander and that don't pay the bills."

"That's a shame. This last room is just a work room. It's used for ..."

"Wow. Now this is a man cave. Got your computer, big screen, easy chair, another great view. Even an exercise bike. I understand this. Ya' come in here and ya' shut the door behind you. No wife to yak at you constantly at the end of the day. No kids hounding you with nonstop, stupid chatter. Close the door and lock it, and that includes the dog. Peace and quiet."

"Peace and quiet?"

"When I work all day, I need a place to escape to where I can be alone. A place where I don't have to listen to another soul say one more word. Yea, I understand what this room's all about. I couldn't face going home if I didn't have mine. All this communication stuff that my wife jabbers about. What is the old saying? Silence is golden? Ain't that the truth? At least that's what I keep telling my family."

"I suppose so."

"I know so. Hey, I wanted to ask you about that vintage VW in your driveway. When I was in high school me and the next-door neighbor..."

Judith Warren

As a Florida resident for thirty years and a high school teacher for most of that, I am also a member of SCBWI as well as FWA. For five years I have met monthly with a critique group and have completed a middle grade trilogy and an animal fantasy.

DAPHNE TELLS ALL

"Hey Stu. Whatcha doin' here? It's early. I'm barely outta bed. And what's with
   the parrot?"

"I'm going away for a while, Danny….a vacation. And I need you to watch Daphne here."

"Awrrk. Let me in, dork."

"I suppose you taught her to talk like that? Does she also curse like you do?"

"I didn't teach her anything. She just hangs around and picks things up. Pretty quickly too. Say, can I use your head?"

"What, you don't have a bathroom at home? And why do you look like shit?"

"Come on Danny. I stopped for breakfast on the way over. And I gotta go."

"Awrrk. Gotta go. Gotta go."

"Jeez, Stu. Is your stupid parrot gonna take a shit here too?"

"Nah. She's pretty well trained. She's just mimicking what I said. Or

207

'parroting me", ya know. That's why they're called parrots."

"OK, OK. Go use the head…So, Daphne, what will you do here while Stu's away? I can't be watching you all the time. I gotta work, and I have a life too."

"Awrrk. What will I do? Sheila's dead. Sheila's dead."

"Whaaaat? What the hell are you saying?"

"Awrrk. Awrrk. Sheila's dead. What will I do?"

"Hey Stu. Hurry up in there. Your parrot's talking crazy."

"Awrrk. Daphne's talking crazy. Sheila's dead."

"Whassup Danny? Don't pay attention to anythin' she says. I have her cage down in my car. Plus a couple bags of food. She won't be any trouble. She'll stay in her cage when you're out. And she doesn't fly. Her flight feathers were clipped."

"I don't care if she flies around. I don't want her taking a shit all around my apartment, Stu. I got a new girlfriend and I'm gonna score with her soon."

"Hey man, bring her over here. Chicks love Daphne. It shows you got a sensitive side, if you got a pet. Plus this place is pretty nice. Just small. I'd put Daphne's cage right over here on the desk."

"So who's Sheila? While you were in the john, Daphne said 'Sheila's dead.' I thought Sheila was your new friend."

"Uhh….Yeah. Sheila was my friend. I mean she *is* my friend. Daphne mighta picked something up from the TV. We were watching old movies last night at my place, Sheila and me."

"So why would Daphne say Sheila's dead?"

"It's not like that Danny. Daphne copies things she hears, but not always together. Ya know? Like somethin' from the movie on TV, followed by somethin' I said, or maybe somethin' Sheila said."

"Awrrk. Sheila's goin' to the cops."

"Stu, you're acting really weird. Why would Sheila go to the cops? What are you into?"

"Don't get all excited. Nothin's goin' on. Don't know where Daphne got that. 'Cept maybe from the movie last night."

"So, what's up with this vacation? Is Sheila going with you?"

"Uhh. Sheila's gotta work. I'm goin' up to the mountains. Maybe do some skiin'. Hang out at this neat resort, catch some babes. Hope there's snow."

"Why would you go to a ski resort if there's no snow? That'd be pretty expensive. Somethin's going on Stu. Whassup?"

"Awrrk. Gotta hide. Hide in the snow."

"There you go Danny. She's not making sense right now. She's combinin' things she's heard in different places. You'll find out if you leave the TV on for her. She'll mix up lotsa stuff that she hears."

"So who's gonna hide in the snow, Stu? Where did that come from?"

"I told ya. She combines lotsa stuff. Don't worry about it."

"Awrrk. Hide in the snow. Hide. Hide the gun."

"A gun. Whose gun? What gun's she talking about, Stu?"

"Musta been something from the TV last night. We was watchin' some old gangsta' movie. I dunno."

"So, how come I didn't know you were going on vacation? I saw you two nights ago and you didn't say anythin'."

"What's with all the questions Danny? It came up kinda sudden. This guy from work has a place near the resort and he said I could use it for a few days."

"What guy? I thought I knew the guys from your job. You mean that new bartender? You hardly know him. Why would he let you stay at his vacation place?"

"He's offered it to a lot of us. I'm just the first to take him up on it. Plus this'll be a slow week, bein' right before Thanksgiving. I wouldn't make a lot of tips anyway. So you'll watch Daphne?"

"This is all kinda strange, Stu. You look terrible, like you're wired, and all this talk sounds like somethin' bad happened."

"Awrrk. Hide the gun. Hide the gun."

"Stu, did you do something with a gun? Are you in trouble? Is that why you're going away?"

"Don't ask so many questions Danny. You sound just like Sheila. 'Where'd that money come from? Whose drugs are those?' I swear she never shut up."

"Oh God, Stu. Are you dealing drugs? You sure look like you're using. Did that guy from work get you involved in it? Is he your supplier? Is that why he's lending you his cabin ... to hide out?"

"Awrrk. Hide out. Hide in the snow."

"Danny, you're just guessing. But don't go there, you're gettin' too nosy."

"Cause you're my friend. I don't want to see you go to jail or nothin'."

"I ain't going' to jail. Nobody can prove anythin'."

"Awrrk. Goin' to jail. Sheila's dead. Sheila's dead."

"Stu, did you have something to do with Sheila bein' dead?"

"Aw, Danny. Don't get involved. She had such a big mouth. She was gonna go to the cops. I gotta protect myself here."

"Awrrk. He's got a gun. Got a gun."

"Put that gun away, Stu. You gotta tell the cops what you know. You can turn in that bartender guy and maybe they'll go easy on you for cooperatin'. I'll take care of Daphne if you go to jail."

"I ain't goin' to jail. I need ta disappear 'fore they connect Sheila to me. I'm goin' upstate where no one will find me. Now I worry about your talkin' to the cops. You don't know how to keep your mouth shut. I can't have that Danny."

"Whhhaat? Why are pointing that gun at me? You're just getting' yourself in more trouble."

"No. I'm getting' myself outta trouble. Sorry Danny, but I can't take a chance on your figurin' out what I done and tellin' the cops. Goodbye friend."

"Awrrk. Gun is loud. Too much noise."

"I guess it's just you and me now Daphne. I'll hafta take you with me after all. You're a big mouth, but who's goin' to pay attention to a dumb parrot?"

"Awrrk. Danny's dead. Danny's dead."

 ## JUDITH WEBER

A retired Real Estate agent, Judy has written two murder mysteries set in St. Augustine, with a Realtor as protagonist. The effort this year is to not only get them published, but to also create compelling short stories that entertain the reader, and perhaps win a place in an anthology.

YEARS

This is the story of the Florida Writers Association's first ten years as told by its founders and members. Starting with a concept of "Writers Helping Writers" shared by a few friends around a kitchen table back in 2001, FWA has grown into a professional organization of more than 1200 members coming from every corner of our home state of Florida, plus twenty other states and the Virgin Islands.

The Florida Writers Association provides the state's largest three-day annual conference for published and aspiring writers, hosts special one-day writers' sessions across the state, offers over forty local writers groups and critique programs, issues a quarterly magazine titled *The Florida Writer*, provides a comprehensive website and online store for products and books written by FWA authors, and maintains a writers' blog. Additionally, members may submit their work to the prestigious Royal Palm Literary Awards Competition each year as well as a contest for our annual themed Collection of short stories.

FWA plays a significant role in developing Florida writers while providing excellent opportunities for publication and strengthening literacy. The story of the Florida Writers Association is still unfolding, but our history to date illustrates what can be done by creative, energetic people with a vision. Visit us at www.FloridaWriters.net.

FWA's Collection #4
MY WHEELS

The next book in FWA's Collection series is FWA's Collection #4 - My Wheels, to be published in the fall of 2012. It's all about wheels. Your first wheels, your favorite wheels, the most unusual wheels, anything with wheels…roller skates, bicycles, motorcycles, cars, trucks, golf carts, wheelchairs, or anything else that comes to mind. You can write true stories about your wheels, or spin a fiction tale. You can share something humorous, or make us cry. It's your choice—it's your wheels!

Watch our website for complete entry guidelines and more details. www.FloridaWriters.net

This short story contest, sponsored by the Board of Directors of Florida Writers Association, and by Peppertree Press, who is the Official FWA Publisher for Collections, was created to offer our members another way to be published, and another way to grow their writing skills.

Each year, the contest has a theme. All writing must conform to that theme, and must be within the total word limitations as set forth in the guidelines. Both fiction and nonfiction are permissible. Even poetry, if that's how your muse moves you.

The annual contests are fun—they give you an opportunity to enter several times with different pieces you've written. They stretch you—giving you parameters and guidelines that you may not have considered or written within before.

All judging is done on a blind basis. Stories are posted by title and number only. The number is assigned consecutively as stories are received. Up to seven judges read each entry entirely and vote according to whether or not it was well-written and struck a chord with them. As with any judging, there is some subjectivity to the process. However, the judges understand that each entry selected as a winner must be ready for printing, as we will do no editing other than fixing minor typos.

Our Person of Renown for this book is a highly-guarded secret. There is no doubt that our Person of Renown is known for their wheels…and will be an instant hit with Florida Writers Association members when we officially kick off this new book on Sunday morning right before closing ceremonies.

Our Person of Renown will roll in, eager to assume the mantle of this special role for the next year. You'll feel, hear, and see the excitement as we rev up for next year's contest!

As in the past, our Person of Renown will select their Top Ten Favorite entries out of the judges' top sixty…and we'll be off and running with another book for the Collection, and another contest to look forward to for the following year.

CPSIA information can be obtained at www.ICGtesting.com
Printed in the USA
LVOW100520071011

249521LV00003B/1/P